PRASE FOR M. [...]

Top 10 Romance of 2012, 2015, and 2016.

— BOOKLIST: THE NIGHT IS MINE, HOT POINT,
HEART STRIKE

One of our favorite authors.

— RT BOOK REVIEWS

Buchman has catapulted his way to the top tier of my favorite authors.

— FRESH FICTION

A favorite author of mine. I'll read anything that carries his name, no questions asked. Meet your new favorite author!

— THE SASSY BOOKSTER, FLASH OF FIRE

M.L. Buchman is guaranteed to get me lost in a good story.

— THE READING CAFE, WAY OF THE WARRIOR:
NSDQ

I love Buchman's writing. His vivid descriptions bring everything to life in an unforgettable way.

— PURE JONEL, HOT POINT

ON YOUR MARK

A WHITE HOUSE PROTECTION FORCE ROMANCE

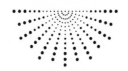

M. L. BUCHMAN

Buchman Bookworks

Receive a free book and discover more by this author at: www.mlbuchman.com

Cover images:

Brown Old Paper © gabyfotoart

French bulldog wearing police harness © lifeonwhite

Children with Dog in Park © jeancliclac

Multiethinic couple piggybacking in city © AlexLipa

Couple Enjoying Camping Holiday © monkeybusiness

Green Grass Backgroud © halina_photo

Declaration of Independence on White House building © izanbar

Other works by M. L. Buchman:

With special thanks to Allyson and Rebecca for connecting me with Shawn Stewart of www.dogsareeasy.com.

Shawn is a top trainer of domestic and police dogs, even working closely with a former First Family's pets. I deeply appreciate his generous time explaining some of the little known details of training and handling detection and attack dogs.

Any mistakes are my own.

CHAPTER ONE

*M*alcolm was happier than a horned toad at a mayfly festival.

And when his English springer spaniel was happy, Jim was happy.

It was one of those impossibly clear days that Washington, DC, dished out like dog treats in February. The chill winter days were probably behind them. In another month, even the occasional below-freezing nights would be nothing but a memory. Now it was an hour past sunrise, the temperature was already above forty, and the maples and beeches along the White House fence line looked as if the tips of their branches had been dusted with just the tiniest bit of bright green. The ornamental cherry trees were already glowing bright pink with the promise of the spring to come.

The air smelled fresh and vibrant with possibility. He loved the way that every city had its own smell. He'd now been in DC long enough that each season wrapped about him like fireflies on a summer evening with its own special particulars. Most of his life had been lived on the road in one way or another, but three years here just might be enough to anchor him in place for a lifetime.

He often wondered what Malcolm smelled on such days. The freshening grass? The latest civilian dog pee-o-gram on a tree trunk? The track of the other US Secret Service PSCO explosives-sniffing dog currently on patrol?

Handling a USSS Personnel Screening Canine—Open Area, also known as a friendly or floppy-eared dog, around the White House perimeter was the best duty there ever was. He and Malcolm had been walking this beat for three years now, putting even the mailmen to shame. Just because a blizzard *and* a hurricane had ripped through last year, each shutting down the city, didn't mean the security at the White House put its feet up—at least not these six paws. The only things that had been moving in the whole area during either event were emergency services, the guards at the Tomb of the Unknown Soldier out at Arlington Cemetery, and White House security.

The snowstorm had been a doozy by DC standards, almost as deep as Malcolm's legs were long. The next morning had been a surprisingly busy day at the fence line as tourists had trudged through a foot of heavy, wet snow to get photos of the White House under a thick, white blanket. Most of the crazies had the good sense to stay warm in their beds that day.

Not even the worst of the crazies came out during the hurricane.

Today it was the sunshine *and* the madness that drew people to his patrol zone along the White House fence. Delineating the two before Malcolm picked out the madness-motivated ones had become one of his favorite games to occupy the time. He figured the visitors to the fence fell into five distinct categories, only two of which Malcolm was trained to give a hoot about.

The True Tourist. They would just stand and stare though

the steel fence. It had been formed to look like the old wrought iron one, but was far stronger—a Humvee that hit this fence would just bounce off. These people were often the older set. They were easily marked at a distance by taking pictures of the White House rather than taking selfies of them *at* the White House.

The Clickbait Tourist. They'd barely glance at the magnificent building. But even if they never actually looked at it, everyone inundated by their social media feeds probably more than made up for the lack.

The Squared-away Vet. The ex-military who arrived to see the representation of everything they had given. Whether standing tall or rolling along in a wheelchair, they came to see, to try and understand. He liked talking to them when he could. Jim had done his dance. Nothing fancy—a "heavy" driver for three tours hauling everything from pallets of Coca-Cola to Abrams tanks.

The Mad Vets and the Crazies. These guys were damaged. The less toxic ones just wanted to tell their story to the President so that he "really" understood. But there was a sliding scale right up to the ones who wanted retribution. These were the fence jumpers. They might have a protest sign, an aluminum foil hat, a .45 tucked in their pocket, or a load of righteous wrath strapped to their bodies. No real plot or plan, they were solo actors and had to be stopped one at a time. He and Malcolm caught their fair share of those—maybe more because Malcolm was such an awesome explosives detection dog. These were the main target of the fence patrol.

The Terrorist. Bottom line, that's why his team and all of the others were here even with them all knowing they were, at best, no more than an early warning of any concerted attack. They'd all seen the movies *White House Down* and *Olympus Has Fallen*. It was amazing how much Hollywood could get wrong and still scare the crap out of you—definitely not entertainment to anyone who worked guarding the White House. They discussed worst-case scenarios all the time. And he sure prayed that it didn't happen until after he was dead and buried—though he'd wager that he could be pissed just fine from the grave if someone attacked his White House. Three years of walking around its perimeter, keeping it safe, made it at least partly his.

It was still early enough in the day that the fence line was almost exclusively the top three categories. The Mad Vets and the Crazies category typically didn't kick in hard until later in the day when their morning meds wore off.

He saw a Squared-away Vet standing at the fence. The officers were particularly easy to pick out. They liked everything in order and would instinctively find the exact centerline—at either Lafayette Square to the north or the curving line of the President's Park to the south like this one. As predictable as sunshine on a clear day, they would come to a halt at precisely the twelve or six o'clock positions and simply stare.

Normally they didn't notice him or react if they did. This one stared at him...no, at Malcolm, with eyes so wide it was a wonder that they remained in his head.

"*Gute Hund,*" he instructed Malcolm—training him in German avoided confusion with an alert word accidentally spoken in a sentence. He'd met a dog once trained with the numbers in Japanese: *Ichi*—sit. *Ni*—stay. *San*—down. *Shi*—heel... Pretty darn slick. He'd thought about retraining Malcolm to be bilingual for the fun of it, but it seemed a dirty trick to play on a perfectly nice dog.

Gute Hund—good dog—told Malcolm he was off duty and could relax and be a dog for a moment rather than a sniffing magician.

It also gave Jim an excuse to let Malcolm approach and really check out the veteran up close just in case he was a Crazy-in-disguise. Even "off duty" Malcolm would respond if he smelled something dangerous.

Nope, guy was clean.

Jim glanced back at his patrol partner and nodded to indicate he'd be stopping for a moment. PSCO dogs never worked the fence line alone. Sergeant Mickey Claremont followed five to ten meters behind him. He was a big guy, looking even more so because of the bulletproof vest over his warm coat clearly labeled USSS Police. The AR-15 automatic rifle that he carried across his chest was part of his primary duty of being backup in case Malcolm did alert to someone. His second job included making sure that nothing slowed Jim's and Malcolm's progress. But Claremont had learned that there were certain types of guys that Jim always stopped for.

"You handled dogs?" He asked the wide-eyed vet hovering uncertainly at the fence.

All he managed was a nod back.

"Been out long?"

Head shake...then a grimace.

"Don't worry about it, brother. The words will come back eventually."

"You sure?" Barely a whisper and now the guy was watching him.

"Three tours in the Dustbowl. Nothing fancy. A heavy driver on the Kandahar and Kabul run." A fellow soldier would know what that meant. Hauling heavy loads, desperately needed by the in-country teams, from the port at Karachi, Pakistan, across a thousand kilometers to Kandahar, Afghanistan, or another five hundred klicks to Kabul. And every millimeter past the southern Wesh-Chaman border crossing or the Torkham one to the north had been run in constant fear of being a giant target on a known road. They'd lost a lot of guys, but he'd made it out in one piece.

"Two tours in Baghdad. One in Mosul," the guy at the fence was back to staring at Malcolm. He reached out a tentative hand as if he was seeing a ghost, but pulled it back before he could test the theory.

"That's some hard shit, brother," Jim wouldn't have wanted that tour any day. "Just give yourself some time."

The guy nodded, almost desperately.

"Hit the support groups," Jim dug out a card from the stack he always carried and handed it over. "These guys saved my ass. Gotta get back to work now. Good luck, buddy. *Such!*" Like *soock* with a guttural German *ck—Seek!* And Malcolm went back to sniffing his way along the fence line. Even letting the guy know that there was such a thing as "getting back to work" would help.

Claremont folded in behind him and worked the second part of his job as they passed more tourists.

"Yes, he's a bomb-sniffing dog." "No, you can't pet him because he's working right now." "Yes, it's okay to take his picture but, no, he can't pose for a picture because he's working right now." And so on in an unending litany.

Jim was so used to it that the silence always seemed wrong after the crowds thinned out at night but the patrols continued.

They were nearing their one-hour limit. A dog's nose only went so long without a break. One hour on, half-hour off. Which was good, that gave him enough time to do the paperwork that was part of being a PSCO handler: patrol reports, daily security briefing, studying the faces of known risk agents and recent threats. A letter writer was usually just that, someone dumb enough to threaten the President's life. Some even put their return address on the envelope. A single visit from the Secret Service was usually enough to scare those dummies back under the wire. But it didn't hurt to have studied their faces in case they transitioned to The Crazies category.

That's when he spotted the sixth type of visitor to the White House fence—The Newbie.

REESE CARVER STOOD at the White House fence and tried to figure out what had changed.

Actually, she knew exactly what had changed, but she couldn't reconcile how different it *felt*. Two years driving for the Secret Service—mostly in San Francisco, LA, and New York. Six months ago she'd grabbed the brass ring and been accepted for the Presidential Motorcade.

When she first came aboard, she'd waited outside the gate in one of the escort vehicles.

Then they'd started bouncing her around: press corps van, support vehicles for carrying the staff who didn't rate a ride in the President's car or one of the spares, then Command and Control while the guys in the back handled route logistics on the fly, and even the front Sweep Car that checked the route out ahead of the Motorcade.

Hazmat had been hard on her nerves because she knew nothing about what those guys actually did.

Watchtower—the ECM or electronic countermeasures vehicle—was capable of suppressing remote explosive triggers. It could also detect incoming threats that used radar or ones that used laser-targeting and jam those as well. It had made her feel like she was constantly the precise target of the attack—even if there'd never been one. Roadrunner was also a mobile cell tower, satellite uplink, and everything else communications oriented, which convinced her she was being *constantly* irradiated. When she asked, the guys manning the vehicle hadn't said the feeling was completely wrong.

She'd even driven Halfback—the lethal Chevy Suburban that carried the Presidential Protection Detail immediately behind the President's limo. She'd liked that one. The agents were armed to the gills, including a pop-up-through-the-roof M134 Dillon Aero Minigun. Could have used that back on the NASCAR racetracks a few times on some of the assholes who thought ganging up to shut out a female driver was good sport.

With all these different assignments, it had gotten to the point where she'd driven every vehicle except for Stagecoach—the Presidential monster itself, also nicknamed The Beast for a reason—and the ambulance that always trailed along behind.

She'd liked driving the unimaginatively named Spares. The two identical copies of the Presidential limousine played a constant shuttle game with Stagecoach so that a terrorist would never be sure which of the three Beasts carried the President and which were the decoys. Any Spare driver worth their salt dreamed of Stagecoach breaking down and the President shifting into their vehicle—which had happened only five times in the last two decades, so the chances were low.

The Secret Service had hundreds of elite drivers, from the San Francisco SWAT team to the Capitol Police of the Uniformed Division. The competition to reach the Presidential Motorcade had been fierce.

Then she'd crossed the Motorcade drivers' "finish line."

Stagecoach.

Just this morning she'd gotten a wake-up call from the head of the Presidential Protection Detail, Senior Special Agent Harvey Lieber.

"Bumping you to driving Stagecoach, Reese. Get your ass in

here." With Harvey, that wasn't some slur because she was a black woman with an ass that she'd been complimented on far too many times. All it meant was for her to get her ass in there. From him she'd take that, but not from any other asshole.

That call had changed the world.

A part of her was ready to do a victory dance.

Reese Carver—the first woman to drive Stagecoach. And a black woman at that. She wanted to do her dance on the heads of every male idiot who said a woman couldn't do it. Every jerk who'd tried to put her down—even after she'd smeared them off the NASCAR track...or maybe especially then. She'd learned the hard way to keep it all inside. Men were expected to brag, but one little smile out of place and it tagged a woman as a bitch. Fine. Whatever.

But the other part of her could only stand and stare at the White House. Next time she drove onto the grounds, it wouldn't be a matter of escorting the President. Next time he'd be riding in *her* car. She'd have his life in her hands.

"What am I supposed to feel about that?" She didn't have a clue.

"First days are always like that," a deep baritone said from close beside her.

"What?" She turned and looked up at the bright-eyed UD smiling at her. The Secret Service Uniformed Division guys always struck her as a little foolish. Didn't they get it? United States Secret Service meant Special Agent. Secrecy. Not parading around Washington, DC, dressed like a cop. They really should be called something else. Maybe—as they *were* standing on the edge of the National Mall—they should rename them mall cops. She liked that. She'd didn't come up with funny things on her own very often, but that wasn't half bad.

"Your first day?" He nodded toward the White House in a

friendly fashion. His smile said that he was completely assured of his own charm. She'd never yet met a man like that who actually charmed her.

"Not even close," she warned him off.

"Oh," his smile didn't diminish. "You have the look."

"What look?" She didn't have a look. No one was supposed to be able to see what she was feeling. She'd learned that lesson the hard way a long time ago. "Like some lost fem in search of a big, strong, handsome man to protect her?"

He laughed. "Like you can see the White House, but it's spooking the crap out of you worse than a mouse at a cat convention. See that a lot on Newbies."

"Not." Keep it short. Make him go away. Nobody saw through her shields—ever. So not allowed. She looked away and down into the big brown eyes of a smiling springer spaniel. He was standing there looking up at her with his tongue lolling out. She reached out to pet him.

And he sat abruptly.

Reese froze.

It was the signal that explosive-detection dogs used to alert their handler that they'd found something. Out of the corner of her eye she saw the backup man shift his grip on his AR-15 semi-auto rifle as he moved for a better angle. Tourists continued streaming by as if nothing was amiss.

She straightened very slowly, keeping her hands in clear view.

The handler was still smiling, though his hand was now resting casually on the butt of his taser. "Been at the range recently? Malcolm will alert to the gunpowder residue on your sleeves and hands."

"Every day before work." She was a driver, not a shooter, but if it came down to it, she'd be ready. "An hour workout, then five magazines at the range."

"I do my workout after my shift."

He definitely had a very nice workout build—powerful without being overworked. But she wasn't real interested in yet another guy staring at her in her workout gear.

"Maybe I need to switch over to mornings. Though Malcolm here likes to start his mornings right off, then nap at the end of the day while I hit the weights."

So, he'd identified her as Secret Service and figured they'd be using the same gym under the nearby headquarters building. Not a giant leap. Despite what some people thought, protection agents' jobs weren't to be undercover in their suits; it was to be so obvious that no one would think of testing their resolve.

She gave him a little credit for not looking away from her face, despite his comment. So he wasn't a complete low-life. His accent said Oklahoma, his smile said self-proclaimed lady killer, but his light brown eyes, with hair to match, were definitely watching her slightest motion in a way that said professional.

"How about handing me your ID slow as a rattler on a winter day."

She unbuttoned her winter coat, then eased open the lapel of her suit jacket. She reached past her FN Five-seveN 5.7mm primary weapon and slipped out her leather Secret Service ID holder. Despite it having her badge and ID, he called it in. That was good—she liked that he was being doubly careful. When he also confirmed her signing time in and out at the range this morning, she was actually impressed. It was far more than she'd expected from a "mall cop" who flashed his charming smile as if it was all the ID he needed.

"Nice to meet you, Clarice Carver. Sorry for the trouble," he handed back her badge holder. The backup guy eased his AR-15, but not completely.

"Reese." She heard the soft click as the backup reset the safety on his weapon. She'd missed it coming off.

"To your friends?" and that smile was back. Asshole apparently thought it was beneath him to introduce himself.

"And my enemies."

"Good to know. You headed in or planning to stand and gawk a while longer?"

"Headed in," she hated that she'd been caught in a moment of weakness and just wanted to get away from him.

"Well, that's fine then. Me and Malcolm, we're at the end of our hour on the fence. we'll go in with you." And he nodded toward the gate another hundred meters down the sidewalk.

Reese tried to figure out how to shed the guy, but couldn't come up with anything.

He tossed a treat to his dog, then scrubbed his fingers into the dog's fur as it crunched happily. *"Gute Hund. Sehr gut!"* He said it in a squeaky high voice that the dog clearly enjoyed, but it made the man sound totally ridiculous—and actually a *little* charming.

Then he spoke to his dog softly. *"Such."*

And the dog changed; they both changed.

The dog rose to his feet and began sniffing his way forward through the crowd. The UD officer stepped out smoothly and the two of them were suddenly all business. His eyes scanned the crowd ahead of his animal, both of them on watch.

The change was almost shocking.

He was still the same guy. Even though she was looking at his back, she could tell by the way the crowd reacted to him and his dog that he was projecting the same easy-going demeanor ahead like a radar sweep. But by the way he moved —just enough on his toes to be ready for a quick reaction, scanning not where his dog was, but looking out and ahead— spoke of a highly trained professional. Even the positioning of his non-leash hand; it swung close beside the taser on his hip with every stride.

"I'm Claremont, by the way," the backup man was on the move as well and was now passing by her.

She fell in beside him.

"Reese Carver," she offered in return, but he just tapped his earpiece. *Right.* He would have been listening in on the same frequency that the dog handler had used. "Is he as good as he looks?" Reese nodded to the team ahead of them.

"Better. Three years on the fence line. Jim and Malcolm have the highest identify-and-capture ratio of any team by a factor of three times." Claremont smiled at her as if he was answering a very different question about just what kind of quarry the handler identified and captured.

Ladies' man. Didn't matter as it had nothing to do with her. It was his three years patrolling the fence that surprised her. If he and his dog were such hot shit, why were they still doing the beat cop routine out in the weather?

JIM WONDERED at just how stupid he'd been. He'd never even introduced himself—as if his mama hadn't raised him right. And now Claremont chatted up the hot Special Agent Reese like they were old pals. He couldn't quite hear what they were saying, but there was no mistaking Claremont's smooth Southern accent that slayed so many of the ladies.

That's when he identified Reese's accent. It was well masked, like she'd worked on it hard, but she was from the Carolinas just like Claremont.

Redneck trucker from Oklahoma didn't stand a chance.

Too bad. Special Agent meant she was good. But there'd also been a small code on her ID that said she was a member of the Presidential Protection Detail. He almost hadn't called in to confirm her identity because it was so unlikely for that to be forged. He finally had, just to see if he could learn anything else about her. No joy. The main desk had merely confirmed she was USSS and even pushing through to the range officer only confirmed that she had indeed logged five twenty-round magazines that morning. But that little code on her ID said that she was beyond exceptional in more than her looks.

Just two inches shy of his own six feet. Pitch black hair that fell straight to scatter over strong shoulders. Her deeply brown skin was smooth and creamy. It was her dark-dark eyes that had been so hard to look away from. There was something about them that both hid and revealed the woman at the same time.

And when she'd pulled back her jacket, he saw her trim waist with enough of a figure to not make the big Five-seveN handgun look ridiculous in her shoulder holster. The weapon said even more about her. What he could see of the handle had the shine that only came from being held for thousands of rounds.

As he'd returned her ID, he'd spotted the shooter's calluses thickening the web between her thumb and forefinger. She looked like everything a man could want and he'd messed it up something awful.

Sadly, it wasn't the first time. Maybe he was losing his touch. When Linda and her dog Thor had joined the White House team last month, he'd done nothing much about it. At least not right off. That had *seemed* like a good idea.

She'd been cute as hell, and he'd entertained a few thoughts. But while he'd been taking his time, she and her dog had gone on to save over sixty lives, including the President's. It was a Secret Service agent's wet dream—making that once-in-a-career save. Then, while he wasn't watching, she'd gone and fallen in love with the chocolate chef, which seemed a little unfair. It was like the Big Guy upstairs was smacking him in the face and shouting, "Wake up, dude."

The last girl to make him even think about wanting the long-haul had been Margarite of the sleek body, long red hair, and a laugh like Christmas sleigh bells. Though she'd hung with him for almost a year, she'd made no secret that her aim was always set higher. "You've walked that fence so long, there's a rut there with your name on it." Margarite had finally latched onto a Congressional aide who—with her street smarts at his side—was now in the running as a Virginia state senator.

He'd had a lot of time to think about it while walking the fence line. The sex had been good and the companionship great. But they'd been on such different tracks. He'd always been content to be who he was and she'd...never been. In the end he'd wished her well, though what he'd really wished was that she was still there beside him when he woke up in the mornings.

Oh well. He figured that, just like Malcolm, he'd keep patrolling ahead and someday he'd catch a scent and track the right lady.

Pity about Reese Carver though. She was quite something. He wondered what it might be like waking up next to her. It was a very nice image.

At the security booth, he and Reese stepped through the door while Claremont waited for the next dog team to come out.

They both showed their IDs and were waved through easily.

So Reese was known. *Of course* she was known. Her code said Presidential Protection Detail. That was a very small, very elite group. Strange that he hadn't seen her walking around. There was no way not to notice her.

IF JIM the dog handler was arrogant, Reese decided that his backup security was perhaps the least subtle guy on the planet. Pleasant, well-trained, and just about everything he'd said could be taken as sexual innuendo. He always said it as if it was a joke—no way to quite take offense despite her sensitivity being set on ultra-high. But it was getting old by the time they reached the entrance to the grounds. What the guy really needed, she decided, was new material.

Once through, Jim waved to a Uniformed Division woman headed out to take his place. She was preceded by a small, brindle-colored mutt. They looked as if they both belonged in suburbia somewhere, but he wore the harness of a USSS dog and his handler was vested and armed.

"Hey, Malcolm," the woman called out to the springer spaniel.

"Hey, Thor," Jim did the same to her dog. The two of them traded smiles as they passed.

Thor? Reese could only shake her head in wonder. That little mutt was the one who'd caught a potential bomber outside the fence and then saved the President's life just last month? Never judge a dog by its stature, she supposed. The female handler followed Thor as he trotted happily out the gate and joined up with Claremont before heading off on patrol along the other side of the fence.

She looked down at Malcolm and silently asked, *Anything you want to be telling me?*

He just wagged his tail at her.

Reese turned for the White House and almost ran over a teen standing there.

"Hi!"

How did some tourist and her Sheltie dog end up on this side of the fence?

Malcolm almost took Reese out as he and the Sheltie rushed to greet each other in the area usually reserved for her knees.

"Hey, Dilya," Jim said from so close over Reese's shoulder that it was all she could do to not jump.

"Hi, Sergeant Fischer."

"You don't call me Jim and I know you're up to something." He sounded just a little too relieved at having an excuse to say his name in front of her. At least he knew he had been a jerk.

"Doesn't replace a proper introduction, Sergeant," she muttered at him. Southern politeness said that you introduced yourself properly when meeting. And, in her experience, it was a bad sign when a guy couldn't be bothered to do that.

He might have blushed at being caught but he recovered fast, making it hard to tell. "Right. Sorry. Reese Carver, this is First Dog Zackie. Zackie, this is Reese," he addressed the Sheltie. Which explained what the dog was doing here.

"Hey," the girl protested.

Jim just grinned. "And this pint-size piece of trouble is Dilya Stevenson."

"Not the introduction I meant," but Reese could see that he knew that. She turned to the kid, "Hi." She never knew what to say to kids.

They would come up when she used to do publicity for her NASCAR sponsor. The boys were easy—they were either young enough to have a crush on her car or old enough to have a crush on a woman who won races in one. The young girls were tricky. They were either some weird mix of shy and tongue-tied that she'd never understood, or chatty-beyond-belief, which she'd both never understood or had time for. A lot of them idolized her as a symbol of all women or all African-American women or...

She was just a girl who'd grown up in a racing family outside Charlotte, North Carolina. They'd lived a five-block walk from the Charlotte Motor Speedway rather than out in the McMansions along Lake Norman with most of the other pro drivers. As a young girl, if she wasn't watching Pop or her brother racing, she was timing their competition or hanging out in the garage or the pits. The school bus never dropped her at home—it had always dropped her at the Speedway's back gate.

This Dilya was the first teen Reese had been near since she'd left racing and joined the Secret Service. Without even racing as a guide, she had no calibration for what the kid could want.

She was mid-teens, with that strung-out look of hitting her growth, though she'd never be tall. Her skin was about half as dark as Reese's own but the tone was different, so not African heritage. Her hair fell in a thick ruffled wave almost to her elbows, but that wasn't her standout feature. It was her eyes. Impossibly green, they assessed Reese as thoroughly as Reese was assessing her. Except she had the feeling that those green eyes could see far deeper into her than the kid was letting on. Or than Reese was comfortable with.

Her parka was bright blue. Her jeans stonewashed. Her boots red cowboy. She also wore a beautiful, hand-knit scarf of brilliant colors.

The three of them—the five of them counting the dogs frolicking up and down the wide, secured street between the EEOB and the White House—headed toward the entrance to the West Wing. Left with no choice except to draft along, she fell in behind them.

Jim wasn't doing a lot to impress her so far.

"Are you on the New York shopping trip?" Dilya slowed down to ask her.

"What trip?" Reese hadn't heard anything about New York.

"Oh. Never mind." Her smile was pleasantly enigmatic.

Staffers were hurrying past. Dilya and Jim walked as if there was all the time in the world. Reese considered moving by them, but that seemed rude, even for her.

She scanned behind her to the fence line and saw nothing out of place. Thor and his female handler, with Claremont in tow, were just disappearing behind a large beech tree, still devoid of leaves. To her right she could catch glimpses of the grounds through the screen of trees: the children's garden, the basketball court, a hint of blue of the swimming pool, and the white facade of the south face of the White House.

When she turned back, Dilya was eying her closely. A Marine in full uniform had come up beside Jim. It sounded as if they were talking football scores. Didn't they get that it was February and the season was over?

"Maybe you both got off on the wrong paw," Dilya must have noticed the direction of her glare. "You know, I just read *Pride and Prejudice*. They hated each other at first but it was just because they didn't know each other."

Reese swallowed hard. She barely knew the story, but it was a romance novel and they only ended one way. No way was this Presidential dog walker going there.

"You better not be saying what I think you're saying."

"What would that be?" The girl practically batted her eyelashes at her in all innocence. Inside the door, Dilya pulled out her security badge, swept it through the turnstile, then flipped the lanyard over her head.

Reese noted that it was an "All Access" badge: Residence, the Oval, Air Force One, even the Motorcade. She knew for a fact that neither the President nor the VP had kids yet, though both wives had just recently been reported pregnant—the security briefing beating CNN by less than an hour.

"Where did you come from?"

"Uzbekistan. At least I think so. I don't really know. I can still speak Uzbek, so I'm guessing I grew up mostly there."

"How did you end up here?" Reese was finding the conversation more than a little surreal. They stepped through the lobby and past the Situation Room entrance, where the Marine peeled off. There was a solid flow of people around them now, all moving fast and with purpose. Normally she'd be in perfect sync with them, but now she was with these slow-moving dog people and felt out of step with herself.

"I walked."

"You walked from Uzbekistan to the White House?" Reese only roughly knew where that was. North and west of Afghanistan?

"No, silly. I would have had to swim the ocean. I only walked to Pakistan."

Jim stopped so abruptly that Reese slammed square into his back. It was like walking into the SAFER barrier that encircled racetracks. The man was impossibly solid. She stepped back, but her nervous system felt as if she'd just been hit with a taser charge. No man should feel so real.

"You *walked* to Pakistan?" Jim was staring down at Dilya.

The teen shrugged.

"Is that hard?" Reese actually made the mistake of engaging him in conversation despite her plan to never waste her time on him again.

"You walked across the freaking *Hindu Kush*?" Jim ignored her and kept his attention on Dilya. "That's worse than surfing in a Texas hurricane."

Reese had heard of those mountains. Okay, that was hard. Beyond hard.

"With my parents, before they were killed. Then by myself until Kee found me." Dilya winced—perhaps at the memory, perhaps at talking about it at all. "Not fun."

"Not fun?" Jim's eyes were wide. "I drove that road nigh on a couple hundred times. It's the worst place I've ever seen to cross."

Reese looked at him again. More change. He'd driven the Hindu Kush a couple hundred times? That meant he'd been in the military, part of the war effort there. So, he wasn't just some dog handler, not if he'd done that.

"We didn't follow roads much," Dilya took a sudden interest in the First Dog, kneeling to comb his fluffy brown-and-white fur with her slender fingers.

"You really went all the way across those mountains?" Jim missed the teen's desire for a subject change.

"To Bati."

"The soccer stadium? The one converted into a US Special Operations fort?"

Dilya stopped fooling with Zackie and looked up at Jim abruptly.

"I delivered some loads there," he explained. "Fuel and food, mostly. Hauled out some pretty shot-up helicopters too."

"I lived there for over two years with my new parents," Dilya's voice was small.

"You were embedded with—" Jim glanced at Reese and snapped his jaw shut.

Dilya shrugged. "They rescued me from the middle of a firefight...and then they kept me." She jolted to her feet and was gone so fast it was as if she'd never been there.

"Bati?" Reese asked as Jim gazed down the crowded hallway in the direction Dilya had disappeared.

"Forward operating base," he spoke as if he stood ten thousand miles away, looking at the scene. "Spec Ops. Very hush-hush. Home to the best team and best pilot of the entire Night Stalkers—that's Army airborne."

Hard to have grown up in Charlotte and not know about the Night Stalkers. They flew overhead all the time on their way between their base at Fort Campbell, Kentucky, and the Special Operations teams stationed at Fort Bragg, North Carolina. They'd done numerous demos at the Speedway before big races. Once even delivering the pace car from one of their big black helos.

"What was the pilot's name?" She wasn't sure why she asked. She'd only ever met one pilot years before, but the woman had left an indelible impression. A female Army helicopter pilot. Reese hadn't even known there were any. Reese *had* spent a really fun one-week stand with her gunner— a macho Latino named Tim Maloney—but it was the woman who stuck in her memory.

"Emily Beale. Most impressive woman I've ever met." Then Jim turned to face her and that Mr. Charm smile was back. "So far."

CHAPTER TWO

*R*eese really didn't need this shit. She strode off along the short length of hallway remaining to reach the Secret Service Ready Room. It was the largest office in the entire West Wing, roughly twenty-five by ninety feet: about three times bigger than the Oval Office. If size implied power, the Secret Service were it.

She'd only been inside a few times. Normally the Motorcade assembled in the garage beneath the Secret Service headquarters five blocks east of the White House. She'd been on the grounds dozens of times, but almost always in her vehicle.

Jim and Malcolm veered off toward one of the jam-packed desks that filled a whole end of the room without even a glance in her direction. She watched out of the corner of her eye as he topped up a water bowl, played with Malcolm for a moment, then gave him some treats before directing him to a doggie bed. The guy sat at the desk and pulled out some paperwork.

Reese felt kind of irked. First no proper introduction, then —she'd thought—they'd been having a nice moment together with Dilya. Only to be followed by him turning all smarmy and now walking away from her as if she was nothing.

She hadn't been too weird, had she? She'd tried to be normal—but since she wasn't, it was hard to pretend. She'd managed a couple of friendly moments... And now the cold shoulder.

Fine!

Because she was female? Or black? Or... Didn't matter to her. No reason to care anyway what some dog handler thought.

She turned her back on him, walked through the briefing area that could seat thirty agents, and headed for the small side-by-side offices at the far end. They defined the dual nature of the Secret Service.

To the left, Captain Baxter, head of White House Detail for the Uniformed Division and Jim the dog boy's boss. To the right, Senior Special Agent Harvey Lieber, head of the PPD—the Presidential Protection Detail. He'd been her boss for over a year now, but with her promotion to driving Stagecoach this morning, their relationship had just changed. She was now his right-hand woman for all things Motorcade. Actually, his left-hand woman, as he always rode in the front passenger seat in any vehicle the President was aboard.

Reese knocked discreetly and waited at the threshold.

No response as he stared at his computer screen.

"Good morning, sir."

Harvey grunted but didn't look up. He was a good-looking guy. Tall, good shoulders, brown hair and eyes almost the same color as the springer spaniel's—easy bet he wouldn't appreciate that comparison. Rumor said he was single, but imagining a woman being up to his demanding standards was hard to do.

Though she *did* like a challenge, there wasn't any spark there for her. Besides, he was her boss and she *wanted*

Stagecoach. He didn't push her hot button any more than mall-cop-turned-dog-walker Fischer.

He'd ridden with her several times, first out at the James J. Rowley Training Center and later in the Motorcade sitting with her in a Spare rather than with the President. At the time she'd thought it was merely odd, not getting that she was being tested to take over the helm of Stagecoach from Ralph McKenna when he retired.

He didn't look up from his screen as he reached out and pounded the flat of his palm against the wall. Not in anger, more as if… Oh, the shared wall with his Uniformed Division counterpart.

"What?" Captain Baxter stepped up close behind her. He was a crew-cut, gray-haired, one-man-army who was a White House institution. He was now on his fourth President as head of the White House UD.

Reese tried to move aside, but the office wasn't big enough to fit the three of them unless she sat down in the one open chair. And Harvey hadn't invited her to do that.

"We—" Harvey finally looked up and blinked at her in surprise. "Where the hell did you come from, Carver?"

"I've been standing here. Knocked and everything, sir."

"Sass." He looked past her at Baxter. "You've seen it?"

"I've seen it."

Reese hadn't, but figured that they'd know that and kept her mouth shut.

"Who the hell thinks these things up?" Harvey continued grousing.

"Not me."

"Doesn't make me feel any better."

After two years in the Secret Service, Reese was used to cryptic conversations, but this was getting awkward.

Then Harvey looked at her and narrowed his eyes. He

squinted at her long enough that she couldn't help herself and spoke.

"What?"

"I'm gonna bounce you out of Stagecoach."

Reese didn't know whether to rage or cry. All she managed was a squeak as she'd just stopped breathing. She'd fought so hard, never really believing that she'd make the goal of being the President's driver—only two or three per decade made the grade—but that hadn't stopped her from gunning for it. And she'd made it only to have it ripped away on her first day?

It wasn't right. It wasn't fair! She'd—

"Just for the next three days, dammit. I've got three drivers out with that bug that's going around and I need a lead for a First Lady Motorcade. President isn't scheduled outside the Oval this week. So stop freaking out and take a goddamn breath, Carver."

She tried, but it wasn't working well. She tried again and managed a wheezing gasp that made Harvey smile and totally embarrassed her.

"Always good to know how bad you want it," Harvey enjoyed rubbing salt in the wound.

She restricted herself to a simple nod of acceptance. That was twice in one day she'd let her feelings show. *Get it together, girl.*

As to how bad she wanted it? There wasn't a single accolade higher than being the President's driver. It was the Daytona 500 and the Cup Series all rolled into one. It didn't have the high public profile, but that had never been what motivated her to drive.

So the First Lady needed a Motorcade? That meant...

Reese decided it was time to prove she wasn't a complete loser.

"Is it the shopping trip?" The girl Dilya had mentioned that.

First and Second Lady both pregnant. Motorcade. It all made sense.

Harvey opened his mouth, squinted at her, then snapped it shut.

Chalk one up on the scoreboard.

Harvey turned to Captain Baxter. "Gonna need your best dog team, too."

Reese caught herself holding her breath again. Please *not* cold-shoulder Jim Fischer. He'd already deemed her too weird. That she knew he was right didn't help. Or maybe he was the one who was too weird with his non-introduction. Hinting she might be the best woman ever, and then just walking away from her cold.

Whatever he was, it was confusing the crap out of her and she wasn't interested in spending another second in his presence.

Captain Baxter didn't hesitate or turn, just calling out loud enough to be heard throughout the long room.

"Fischer! Get yourself over here, boy."

JIM WONDERED what he'd done wrong this time. Baxter was fussier than his own sister on prom night about getting everything downright perfect. An old warhorse like Captain Baxter fussing with his makeup—now there was an image.

Of course, Jim had witnessed far too many breakdowns, accidents, and just plain damn foolishness while driving the nation's highways—and the Paki-Afghani ones. He agreed with Baxter about getting it all right, but he'd thought he was running clean.

He flashed a *stay* sign to Malcolm as he shoved out of his chair and headed over to the Captain. Malcolm stayed on his doggie bed, but Jim could feel the spaniel's eyes tracking him across the room.

Reese Carver stood there beside the Captain.

Crap! Had she seen something and made a report? Griped about him double-checking her ID? He'd already received the "go away, boy" message loud and clear. He wasn't sure quite what he'd done to make her stalk off like that, but he knew when to steer clear. Apparently not soon enough. He shouldn't have even walked with her through security.

He thumped Thompson, one of the other dog handlers, lightly on the shoulder just to steady himself. Thompson's "Hey, Jim," sustained him most of the way over.

Reese had shed her heavy winter coat and now stood in a typical, dark gray Special Agent suit. Except *typical* had nothing to do with how it looked on her.

He barely managed to stop the whistle of surprise. He'd thought she was hot when all he'd seen was her face. That brief glimpse of her figure as she'd handed over her ID wallet hadn't prepared him for the woman standing here now. She looked dangerous, powerful, and sexy as a centerfold all at once. How did a woman do that?

She glared at him like he was a preacher man for the anti-Christ. He did his best to stop admiring her figure, but it was hard—real hard. She looked sweeter than a hot rod and more powerful than his old Kenworth T680 semi-tractor.

"Yeah, boss?" He focused on Captain Baxter's ugly mug. Far safer.

"Pulling you off the fence."

Jim shrugged his acceptance, but didn't like it. They'd offered him other jobs before, and he'd always found a way to turn them down. This one wouldn't be any different. He liked his walks with Malcolm. He'd seen what happened to other guys who aspired to more. They spent their days patrolling the insides of convention centers and meeting rooms, basement kitchens and garage entries.

Not for him.

Not for Malcolm. Dogs were supposed to be outside with room to roam.

"What is it with you people today?" Harvey growled.

Jim did his best to fix his expression. It was never a good idea to be upsetting the head of the Presidential Detail.

"You two bozos know that First Lady Anne Darlington-Thomas and Former First Lady Geneviève Matthews work for the UNESCO World Heritage Centre at a very *senior* level?"

He didn't pause long enough for either of them to respond, which was fine. He knew it, and if Reese was PPD, she'd certainly know it as well.

"Normally they travel from their offices here in the East Wing up to the UN building in New York about once a month for meetings. Well, this time they've added on a day of shopping, eating out, and going to a Broadway musical. Second Lady going along for the ride." Harvey rolled his eyes as if he was in pain. "The three ladies together will make a very attractive target," then Harvey stabbed a finger in his direction. "Not a single snide remark out of you."

He held up his hands palm out declaring his innocence, though the man was right. First Lady Darlington-Thomas was a short, pretty-as-could-be blonde from one of the best Southern families—with all the class and none of the expected attitude. Former First Lady Ms. Matthews was a tall, full-figured French-Viet beauty who could have had a career walking runways. Second Lady Alice Darlington was just cute as kittens—and a brilliant CIA analyst. The three together would be a total knockout.

And a very high-value target to some nutcase.

Jim glanced at Reese, offering a smile about just how funny

the moment was, but all he got back was the chill professional in her Special Agent suit. Right, she was ready to scrape him off the bottom of her shoe like some of Malcolm's... Jim sighed. Yep, just like that.

Baxter at least offered him a sly grin of commiseration. Whether for Harvey's remark about the leading ladies or Reese's cold shoulder, he couldn't tell.

"They hit the Downtown Manhattan heliport in twenty-six hours. I'll get a logistics team on it, but NYPD is holding a big explosives detection exercise and are reluctant to pull any more dog teams than they have to. I promised to loan them a lead team. So, I want you two in the First Lady's Suburban and headed north now. You can drive there faster than I can get air transport in place. Route and area familiarization today. Pick them up at ten hundred hours tomorrow morning for a day in the city. UN meetings on Day Three, then home that night. I'll have a list of their planned stops before you get there. The rest of the team will be dispatched out of the New York office or fly in with her. You can buy a toothbrush and a change of underwear on the way. Now move."

Harvey Lieber had barely paused for a breath in the whole rundown.

"Well? Why are you two still cluttering up my office. Go!"

So much for even having a moment to blink.

"Let's hustle," Reese turned for the door, grabbing her coat on the way.

"Okay if I get my dog and jacket first?"

Reese made a show of checking her watch, then smiled at him—almost. "Only if you hurry."

It was a nice almost-smile, so maybe he hadn't been totally tagged as an asshole. That would be good as it looked as if they'd be rubbing shoulders for the next sixty-plus hours.

Jim grabbed Malcolm's emergency go-bag: dog food, water

bowl, and doggie med kit. He snagged his full vest, which included his own med kit and extra rounds, then raced for the door with Malcolm at his side. He had to double back for his jacket.

JIM HAD SEEN the First Lady's Suburban before, a carefully unremarkable vehicle. Unlike the President's limo or one of the black-on-black escort vehicles, this was a pleasant bronze color. It was also armored and powerful, with tinted windows and a luxury interior. The back seats had been replaced by a pair of generous arm chairs at the rear and a pair of rear-facing narrow bucket seats forward for aides. It was a serious machine even without its lethal escort.

"Do it," Reese's soft-spoken command echoed in the low-ceilinged garage beneath the Secret Service Building. She nodded to Malcolm. So, her first words since leaving the White House were to his dog. He sighed.

"*Such!*" Jim told Malcolm.

Malcolm circled the Suburban in moments. Jim popped the doors and Malcolm managed to jump in without help despite the high step. In moments he'd sniffed over the interior as well. Other than the two weapons' caches built into the driver and passenger doors, he didn't find anything. He finally curled up on one of the seats and resumed his nap.

They were out of DC and on the B-W Parkway headed north toward Baltimore before he braved her silence.

"Sorry for not introducing myself."

Nothing.

"How long are you planning to hold that oversight against me?" Maybe the problem was that she was distracting as hell. Women had never made him tongue-tied before, but he'd sure messed up around Reese. He *knew* that he'd seen her having a Newbie moment at the fence as clear as bluebells on the Oklahoma prairie, though it still puzzled him. He was finding her harder to read with each passing moment.

Five or six miles rolled by before she responded.

"You're the kind of asshole who thinks that women aren't up to your standard. I can hear the Okie in your voice. You just a misogynist or are you a racist, too?"

"I'm—" He glanced at Reese's profile. It was one of those trick questions with no right answer. He'd never been accused of either one before and he didn't know what to do with it. Denying it wasn't the answer either, because of course that was expected.

"Yeah, that's what I thought."

That finally pissed him off. "You a lesbian bitch or do you just hate dog owners?"

"I'm not—" Then she stopped for a long moment before she snapped out a bark of bitter laughter acknowledging the trap. "Okay, you got me." She slipped through three lanes of traffic in one smooth move.

Another couple miles passed by in strained silence.

"Look—" "Listen—" they both spoke at once as they passed the Fort Meade exit. Rather than go through the whole you… no, you…then more silence scenario, he just plunged in.

"You're driving the First Lady's vehicle."

Reese still didn't glance away from the road.

"You aren't looking real happy about it."

That at least earned him a shrug.

"Why? It strikes me as pretty damned impressive."

Her hands had tightened enough on the Suburban's steering wheel that he could imagine the leather creaking under the strain.

"Okay. Fine. Don't tell me. Can we at least get some

munchies? It doesn't feel like a road trip without Fritos and root beer."

"I don't want to delay getting to New York. There's a lot of ground to cover there before they arrive. Besides, you call *that* road trip food?" At least she was talking.

"Yep! The best." He put on his best hick accent. "I've done driven a couple hundert thousand miles or more jes' on that for fuel. Way-ell…that and a passel o' diesel go-juice. What about you, little lady?"

"Krispy Kremes and Cheerwine."

"Damn, woman. You travel on that sugar rush, you oughta be sweeter than you're being." Cheerwine was a sickly sweet, hyper-carbonated soda from North Carolina. Though he could have thought of a better way to say that, but that train had left the station so it seemed best to just let it go on by.

"And you oughta be more intelligent, but you aren't."

Again the silence dragged out right through Baltimore and onto I-95.

Reese Carver wasn't fitting neatly into any of the types that women always seemed to run into.

Roadhouse Girls were the ones who hung out at truck stops. Not the working girls, but rather the locals looking to be a little bad with a passing trucker. He'd certainly had his fair share of those back in his driving days, but had lost interest soon enough. Got to the point he'd rather just have a good night's sleep.

One step up were the Bar Chicks, looking to find some adventure between the sheets for a night or a week. Like the tackiness of bar floor on a boot heel, they always wore off even when he tried to hold onto one. Maybe faster when he did try.

The Show Girls were damn nice to look at and wholly untouchable. Convinced they were out of the league of everyone around them, and probably right about that.

The Nice Ones were hard to find. Girl next door. High school sweetheart. Stacie had been a nice one. She'd ridden as a shooter on his HETS—heavy equipment transport system, basically a damn big truck for hauling tanks around. They'd shared the route and a whole lot more for six months. But her tour had ended while his military career was just gearing up. She'd saved them both the pain and Dear Jim'd him on their last night together in Karachi.

The Pros. Again, not the working girls. These were the ones all bound up in their careers. They stuck, sometimes for a long while like the sultry Margarite. But they were always looking for what was next.

The Keepers…well, they were a myth of the highway. He saw them but, sure as Christmas falling in December, they were already taken.

Reese Carver was none of those. She had the career focus of the Pro, the iron wall and incredible looks of a Show Girl. But she had the feel of a Keeper without also being a Nice One, a combo he'd never thought of before.

One more try, then he was going to give up. Mama always said that taking problems head-on was better than tackling tapioca—not that he ever knew what she meant by that.

"I still don't know what I did to piss you off."

Reese's hands were hurting from how hard she was gripping the steering wheel, which wasn't a good thing. A light grip was the secret to a good reaction time, but she couldn't seem to ease up.

"You want a list?"

In her peripheral vision she could see Jim shrug as if he didn't care.

Why had he really pissed her off? This wasn't like her.

She knew she was being nasty. It was a defense mechanism that she'd learned the hard way. Enough guys at the track had thought they could get away with grabbing her butt or breast because she was a black woman in a white man's sport. She'd never really noticed before, but it had made her tough. She learned young to be fast with a lug wrench—all that had saved her from a couple of really bad moments that she didn't want to remember.

But when had hard become nasty? She was never rude unless it was called for. Silent, yes. Obnoxious…

"You know Dilya?" Reese had found the best way to win was to slip up on someone sideways—though she didn't know why she'd started there.

"Thought I did. Walked across the Hindu Kush? She was probably at Bati when I was there. Guess I don't know her so much."

"She said something," and Reese couldn't believe she was about to repeat it, but it seemed she was. "About us being like the couple in *Pride and Prejudice.*"

"So I'm the prejudiced jerk and something has wounded your pride?"

"You know the story?" She didn't, but that made sense with the title.

"Sure. Keira Knightley. I'll watch almost anything with her in it."

Which might explain his earlier brush-off. Reese couldn't help glancing down at her own chest. She was no stick-thin, flat-chested white chick. But if that was the way his tastes ran, then why had he been all Mr. Charm and smiles out at the fence?

"Can't say as it fits me," Jim continued. "Don't see myself as much prejudiced against anyone, excepting maybe the folks that tried to kill me overseas. What are you being prideful about?"

Reese sighed. Their stretches of silence had only gotten them through the first hour of the four-hour drive. They'd probably be tied at the hip for several days. Uncomfortable stony silence was still an option…just not a good one.

"Okay," Reese decided to face the real problem. "This morning, I get a wake-up call from Harvey Lieber that I'm taking over as driver for Stagecoach."

"Holy shit!" Jim twisted to face her. "You're the one they tapped to replace Ralph McKenna? The man is a freaking legend. That would scare the crap out of me too."

"I'm not scared." She *absolutely* wasn't scared, even if she'd been momentarily paralyzed at the fence line this morning. That *wasn't* fear, it was…something else. "I fought hard for that job. It's what happened next that is making me crazy."

"You're suddenly driving the First Lady's Suburban on a New York shopping trip," he said with an unexpected insightfulness for someone she'd accused of being an idiot.

Reese sighed. That was it.

"So, you're not only good enough for Stagecoach, but you're good enough to be bounced into the First Lady's vehicle on no notice. Strikes me as winning first *and* second prize at the county fair."

She hadn't thought of it that way. Now she was feeling foolish that she hadn't, yet this Okie dog handler did.

Reese actually glanced away from the road for the first time to look at him. Jim was back to watching the road, not her.

He was squinting ahead, but didn't seem to be looking at the traffic.

"Clarice Carver," he said her name slowly.

"*Reese.*"

"Clarice Carver," he ignored her. "Used to be a NASCAR

driver with that name. I seem to recall she was lighting up the track something fierce, then she just disappeared one day."

That was a past, a moment in time she didn't want to remember.

"Always figured you'd had kids or something."

Or something. No way was she going to be telling this guy about the worst day of her life.

"Used to follow NASCAR pretty close, before I went overseas. You did most of your racing while I was out and gone. Heard you were good though."

"I was the best."

It was like the woman snapped back into focus in that instant. She didn't move, frozen hard at the steering wheel, staring out at the traffic, but Jim could suddenly see her clearly.

Maybe it was the pain in her voice.

Jim needed to call his sister. Sissy was always the red-hot NASCAR fan and could give him chapter and verse on every driver better than Pastor Daniels of Purcell, Oklahoma, First Baptist could quote from his Bible.

Didn't matter though.

"NASCAR to driving the President's limousine. I am sittin' here in the presence of greatness." What the hell kind of internal drive had it taken to do that? The kind that Margarite of the long red hair had always accused him of lacking.

No wonder Reese didn't have time for someone like him. She'd seen right through him and had practically been screaming to be left alone the whole morning. He hadn't done that real well either. He supposed now was as good a time to start as ever.

He glanced into the back of the Suburban.

Malcolm was snoozing and shedding in the First Lady's seat. He'd have to remember to wipe that down before they met the flight tomorrow morning.

Jim turned back to the road and flexed his hands. Even though he was a dog handler now, he'd spent so many years as a truck driver that sitting in the passenger seat felt completely useless.

He didn't even have road munchies to keep his hands busy at something.

CHAPTER THREE

*R*eese was exhausted.

Wake-up call at six—with all of the emotional charge of being named to take over Stagecoach. Then the crash of thinking she was being bounced back out. On the road by eight, and hitting New York City by noon.

Harvey had sent a list of five stores, two restaurants, and a Broadway theater right on Times Square.

She'd dropped Jim at each place, where he and Malcolm had been met by an agent from the New York office familiar with the locale. While he'd been doing site familiarization, she'd scouted approach and getaway routes, driven in and out of garages until she knew the best access to each exit, including where to go to ground if they had to abandon the vehicle.

There was an odd congruency of knowing that Jim and Malcolm were doing exactly the same thing on the other side of the walls. Now that they were separated, they finally made sense together—working as a team to ensure their protectees' safety.

They certainly hadn't made any sense on the drive up. She

supposed she'd gotten what she'd asked for. After unearthing her past, he'd been kind enough to finally leave her alone. Leave her alone to wallow in the pain of events she'd spent the last two years trying to forget.

At the end of the evening, they'd sat together in the car watching the patterns of movement as the Broadway show let out. How the crowd dispersed under normal conditions. Where the limos lined up. How many cabs sat in the queue.

Just on spec, they poked through the local bars and found one that seemed likely if the ladies wanted a drink afterward. The Rum House was a few blocks back from Times Square and didn't have the hard-packed, post-theater draw of Sardi's or Carmine's right on the Square.

"Can I buy you a round?" It was the first non-business thing Jim had said since Wilmington, Delaware.

"As long as the place has food," she'd had a knockwurst with sauerkraut from a street vendor about a thousand hours ago. The only one who'd eaten regularly had been Malcolm. It was nice watching how thoroughly Jim took care of his dog.

"Actually," he was studying the menu mounted by the door, "it does. Not much, but I'm past caring." It was the first hint he'd given that he wasn't utterly tireless in the pursuit of his duty.

He held the door for her, an unexpected politeness, then whispered as she passed close beside him.

"Watch this. It's always fun how these crowds react."

So Reese stepped in and waited. Jim indicated a small table by the window that would let them both sit with their backs to the wall: one facing into the bar, the other facing the window where they could keep an eye on the street.

He nodded for her to go grab the table. Only when she was seated and watching him did he start moving. But he didn't head straight for her. Instead, he guided Malcolm on a curving route that took him much more deeply into the crowded bar. It was quiet with the warm buzz of friendly conversations over soft, piped-in jazz.

While she watched, she decided that this place was a good choice. The Rum House felt upscale Old West. Worn hardwood flooring, heavy on the walnut and mahogany woods for décor, along with benches covered in dark leather and comfortable seats. The old-timey feel was achieved without being all phony about it. Hurricane-style lamps and circular styling of the woodwork simply evoked the era without getting cliché.

It took her a moment to see what was happening with Jim and Malcolm. Urban hipster couples would glance at the dog. Then look away. Then look back and up to see the tall, broad-chested handler. Some would go back to their meals. If it was a group of women however, their gaze intently followed Jim.

Had she really not noticed how handsome he was? And in this crowd, his good-old-boy attitude really stood out. Mr. Tall and Easy-going in his dark blue jacket with USSS emblazoned across its back in six-inch yellow letters. She'd never managed easy-going for a single second of her life, yet he looked as if he'd never been anything else. She could almost admire that.

Reese recalled their one actual contact, when she'd run into his back outside the West Wing Secret Service Ready Room. When he'd felt so impossibly solid and real. His long silences on the drive up had been uncomfortable at first, but by the end of it, she'd started to take on a little of his silence as her own. She wasn't used to that and couldn't decide if it was all bad or not.

Was the reaction of the women what Jim wanted her to see? Mr. *Guy* showing off how male he was?

Then he got a new reaction from a couple laughing over drinks.

Dog—turn away—Jim—turn away...

Then a double take so hard that the couple almost fell out of their chairs. The instant Jim was past them, they jolted to their feet without finishing their drinks. The man threw some bills on the table as if they burned him and then the couple raced for the door.

Jim didn't turn to follow their hurried exit; instead he shot her a big smile with a silent laugh behind it. At the far end of his wandering loop, he turned for her, continuing his wandering way through the crowded tables.

A group of three guys at a nearby table had the same massive double take-and-bolt reaction the moment they spotted Jim. No, the moment they spotted Malcolm.

This time they were close enough that she could see their faces go sheet white before they ran. One of them, while dumping bills on the table, accidentally tossed down a baggie of white powder. He looked at it in horror, then at Jim's back. He almost snatched it up, then, thinking again, he left the baggie on the table and ran out the door as if all the hounds of hell were after him rather than a sweet little springer spaniel who hadn't even looked at him twice.

Jim dropped into the chair beside her and Malcolm sat by his side. Jim wasn't laughing out loud, but he looked awfully pleased with himself.

Reese couldn't help herself and let the laugh out. After all the craziness and stress of the day, it was great watching people who didn't know that an explosives-sniffing dog wasn't trained to react to illegal drugs.

She laughed until it grew all out of proportion. It was like a release of so much she'd been keeping under hard control. She was going to be chauffeuring the three leading ladies of the current administration, and these people were freaking out about whether they'd be caught for having a couple hundred bucks of cocaine in their pockets.

Jim didn't look worried, he just waited her out until she could catch her breath.

JIM COULDN'T CATCH his own breath. He'd never imagined that the impossibly serious Reese Carver of the Presidential Protection Detail could laugh—and definitely not like that.

She was undone, and a shockingly beautiful woman emerged into clear view, no longer hidden by the serious, kick-ass heroine that would do just fine facing down Batman or Superman...or both at once. A stunning, black Wonder Woman in US Secret Service armor. All she needed was a sword and golden lasso of truth to complete the image.

Had *he*, with his little dance about the room, made her laugh like that? It did sound as if she was laughing with him and not at him, which struck him as encouraging—even if it was all out of proportion with the joke. He rubbed Malcolm's head to give her a moment.

Reese wiped at her eyes with a napkin and took quick sips from a glass of water that a waiter had rushed over.

Good service, another important aspect of choosing a locale to bring the First Lady's party tomorrow night. He'd also liked that the bartender working nearest the door was built like a bouncer and had traded a quiet nod of acknowledgement with Jim when he'd spotted the USSS on Jim's jacket. Subtle but watchful. Jim looked over at him while Reese finished her recovery. The bartender offered him a quick smile, clearly appreciating the joke as well.

A waitress cleared the abandoned tables, looking pleased at the generous payments dumped on each table. She delivered the baggie of powder to the bartender to deal with. The man grimaced, glanced one last time at Jim for saddling him with how to explain it to the police, then turned back to his other business.

"Thanks," Reese's voice was rough with the laughter, as if there had been pain behind it as well. "I guess I needed that."

"If you had told me before that you could laugh like that, I'd have no more believed you than a bright purple pinto horse."

"If I had told *me* I could laugh like that, I'd have called me a liar. Been a long time."

"Want to talk some about it?"

"Definitely not."

He ordered an Oklahoma Tropical Twister and she ordered a North Carolina Rum Cherry Bounce. The waitress was good; she didn't blink once at the two strange requests that had nothing to do with the big bad city. A pair of grilled Gruyère cheese sandwiches and a couple of sliders for Malcolm, without the buns or condiments, completed their order, and then they were alone again.

Still she wasn't talking, but he didn't want to let the moment go. It had been the first crack in the ice wall.

"Strange day," he started.

Reese offered a shrug of agreement.

He needed a new topic, without sounding like he was fishing. But he wasn't having much luck finding it.

"How did you get into dogs?" Jim could only blink in surprise at the sudden opening. All day, dark shades had hidden her eyes and her thoughts. Now the dim lighting of the bar seemed to do the same. Unable to read why she'd asked, he was still glad for the opening—surprisingly glad for it. It was clear that she was something special and, without him noticing, the brush-off had hurt. He knew he was good at what he did, but not being good enough for Reese Carver hurt.

"Mom gave me a German shepherd pup for my tenth birthday. I had to train him fast if I wanted to ride with Dad during the summers." He scratched Malcolm's head where it rested on Jim's knee.

"Ride with Dad?" Reese's tone could have been for a job interview. Very matter-of-fact and to the point. Maybe that was just the way she rode.

"He's an over-the-road owner-operator."

"You say those words as if they mean something," Reese said it deadpan with neither tease nor irritation. She was so neutral that she almost disappeared back behind her hard shell again.

"Long-haul trucker, which they call over-the-road. Owner-operator means that he's an independent who owns his own rig. Actually he owns nine of them. Now that us kids are all grown, Mom runs the business from the passenger seat—though she drives some too. My brother, sister, and two first cousins all drive for him."

"But not you?"

"Did local delivery during high school summers and long-haul a couple years after, once I was old enough to get my commercial ticket." Those had been good years. He wasn't sure why he hadn't gone back to them. Mom and Dad had found a lifestyle on the road that fit them, but he hadn't.

He told her how they stayed in touch despite the entire family's mobile lifestyle. He'd get a call every time someone in the family had a run that hit DC and they'd get together for a meal. Just last June, everyone had runs that hit Roanoke, Virginia. He and Malcolm had gone over for a couple days and they'd made a reunion out of mini-golf, BBQ, and some tall cold ones.

"Then the dogs," Reese interrupted his memories.

"Then the Army. Drove HETS—that's Heavy Equipment Transport System."

"Don't know those either."

"Big trucks. Seriously big," he liked sitting with her as if they did this all the time.

"You're a trucker kind of guy," Reese concluded and went silent as if the interview was now over.

"Was. Now I'm a dog kind of guy."

"Makes you the black sheep of the family," she nodded once to herself. She now had him well pigeonholed. He didn't know if that was comforting or irritating.

"Black dog—or brown-and-white in Malcolm's case—but yeah. How about you?"

———

How about her? Reese's past was a complete train wreck compared to Jim's ever-so-happy trucking family—*all for one and one for all.*

The waitress' delivery of their drinks bought Reese a few moments. The waitress guaranteed herself a nice tip by bringing out a water bowl for Malcolm.

Sipping the sweet rum cocktail that tasted a lot like home bought her a few more moments.

Like home.

That was all gone. Charlotte. The Motor Speedway. Her family.

"That was one dark thought," Jim was seeing past her armor once again.

She felt the automatic brush-off shrug ripple across her shoulders...and didn't like it. What was it about herself that she couldn't just talk to someone? She'd never known how to do that when she was a racer and she hadn't become any better at it in the Secret Service. Always a loner, just a highly skilled one.

For once, she was sitting next to someone who she *wasn't* in competition with. He was a nice guy, a dog handler, and *wasn't* after the same job she was.

"Okay, fine!"

"Fine?"

"I meant that for myself. I drove NASCAR."

"Already figured that." But he said it nicely.

"Made it to second row starting position. My dad had the fastest qualifying time for the race, so it was hard to feel bad about not getting the lead on the start. We started our last race at the head of the field; Number One and Two in a field of forty-three." She couldn't look up at Jim, instead seeing the heat shimmering off the Motor Speedway. A one-and-a-half-mile oval, it was going to be fast with the warm track giving the tires good traction. Turn 4 was in the shade of the grandstands. It would be slicker just at the moment that they transitioned from blinding afternoon sun coming out of Turn 3, plunging into the relative darkness of the shadowed Turn 4.

Every driver knew, and they were ready. That was where the accidents were going to be happening that day.

"I watched—"

Reese had never told anyone about this moment. Not the reporters, not the Secret Service interviewers.

"We were still running one and two after fifty laps. I was a car-length back when Pop lapped someone, or tried to. They banged fenders. A nothing contact. Such a little bump. But it was just enough to break his front end loose going into Turn 4."

She'd been drafting so close that she could see his face as the car spun a one-eighty. For just an instant he was traveling backward into the turn at a hundred and eighty miles an hour

—nose to nose with her car. NASCAR racers rode the ragged edge of aerodynamically stable when they were nose into the wind.

"The wind caught the tail of his car. One moment he was right there in front of me," Reese looked out into the bar but all she could see was the track. "The next, he was tossed twenty or thirty feet into the air, slamming into the high fence. Flipping and spinning like a toy even worse than Richard Petty's historic crash."

A warm, strong arm across her shoulders was all that let her speak. All that let her breathe. She was caught up in the retelling and couldn't find any way out of it other than through.

"They have safety flaps in the roof that are supposed to break up the effect, but a weakened hinge broke and it didn't break up the unwanted lift. I got away clean, ducking under the wreck while it killed my father."

She sat up abruptly and faced Jim.

"I kept it cool. I ran safe and clean. Even when the pit boss came on the radio to tell me he hadn't survived, I held my line and raced. Some idea that I was going to win it for Pop."

"Did you?" His voice was a close whisper of sympathy.

She shook her head. "Blew an oil ring with ten laps to go. Engine tossed a rod and I was out. It happens."

Jim held her close. It felt so good to be able to turn into his shoulder and just be held.

Thankfully she'd buried the worst thing from that day so deep it didn't come out.

"My baby brother, always a little wild, died in the Argentine desert during the Dakar Rally. Pop died on the Charlotte Motor Speedway—his home track. I decided that I wasn't going to die there."

"What about your mom?"

When she tried to knock back her entire drink, Jim slipped it out of her hand and set it back on the table next to his own. Didn't matter. She drank so little that even half a drink had gone straight to her head, or why would she be telling a jerk of a stranger all that she was telling him?

"She was the smart one of the family. She left when I was three. Pop said she married a schoolteacher in Oregon. Didn't even call for the funeral."

Jim Fischer waited while alcohol, shame, and chagrin washed through her system like a bad fishtail. Waited while she stared at the tabletop as her heart threatened to throw a rod through her chest and end her. Finally she just stared at her fisted hands on the table.

Something bumped against her thigh a couple times on the side away from Jim, then a weight settled there. She looked down in surprise to see Malcolm looking up at her with sympathetic doggie eyes. Reese rubbed his head and felt a tiny bit better.

"HE SEEMS TO LIKE ME."

"He has good taste in women."

Reese looked at him with surprise in her eyes.

"Not me," he held up his hands. "I have terrible taste in women. I always end up with the 'just friends' type." Now why had he paid her a compliment? She'd been hard-edged and pushing him away all day. And here he was handing her some cheap line. Except it didn't *feel* like a cheap line. She *was* an amazing woman, just not the type he ever landed.

"Just friends," she sounded thankful for the change of topic.

"Sure. Not a one of them has ever knit me a sweater."

Reese just blinked at him.

He took a bite of his sandwich, which had arrived at some point without his quite noticing. He looked down at the floor and saw that Malcolm had polished off his sliders *before* going to console Reese. He picked up the empty plate and slid it under his.

Reese Carver. She'd seen some seriously harsh times. Alone in the world, no wonder she'd brushed him off. He'd be scared to death of getting close to anyone again—the loss must have been horrific. Well, he might not understand how hard she'd brushed him off, but at least it explained things a bit.

He nudged her plate toward her. She nodded at it, but didn't take a bite.

"Ma always said that you could tell if a girl was serious if she knit you a sweater."

"I don't knit," Reese finally reached for her late dinner, keeping a hand on Malcolm's head.

"Ma either, but she swears it's true."

"So, I guess we're never going to be serious."

"Guess not." He knew he was out of the running, but he did wonder if Malcolm was going to get lucky tonight. He knew from experience that sad doggie eyes earned him a portion of almost any woman's dinner. Margarite had had no willpower where Malcolm was concerned. Jim had to admit that even being a long-time dog person, Malcolm could almost get by his own guard with that act.

Reese took a bite of her sandwich, then set it back on her plate without offering any to Malcolm.

He heaved out a doggie sigh and looked across her lap at him for aid in his nefarious plans. Jim simply shook his head, which earned him another doggie sigh.

He wasn't sure where to take the conversation from here.

He'd painted himself into a corner by bringing up relationships, which would be more likely with one of the people still streaming by on the sidewalk—despite the late hour—than with Reese Carver.

She was clearly done with the topic of her life after her cathartic upheaval. No tears. Not her. Never her.

"When did you learn to be so strong?"

That earned him a bark of laughter sharp enough to startle Malcolm.

"What?"

Reese opened her mouth, closed it again, and turned back to her sandwich. Malcolm did eventually get the tail end of a crust with a little cheese on it, but far less than his normal take. Reese was made of sterner stuff than most.

The crowd inside still wasn't thinning. The waitress swept up their empty plates and set down a dessert menu. Neither of them was more than half through their drink, so she slipped off to thirstier clients. Nearing midnight, it really was the city that never slept. Most of his New York trips had been to one loading dock or another. The tourist center of Manhattan wasn't a place he'd ever had to run an eighty-foot full-box rig, and riding shotgun with Reese all day had convinced him that he'd never want to try.

Tomorrow was going to be a long hard day. By unspoken mutual consent, they both clambered to their feet and shrugged on their jackets. He paid the bill and they drove across town to the hotel near the UN. A location team from the New York office was already on patrol there and nothing remained except to check in and ride up in the elevator.

At the door to her room, she stopped him before he could lead Malcolm to the next room down the hall.

"You know that you're pissing me off, Fischer?"

"Kind of hard to miss that."

She shook her head and her long hair was lustrous beneath the soft lighting of the long corridor.

He waited.

"You're making me think. I don't like thinking."

"What do you like?"

"Winning," she didn't hesitate a single moment. Then her voice went much softer. "That's what I've always been good at anyway."

"Doesn't sound like a bad thing."

"No… But it's a pretty damn lonely thing. Pop was dead—and I raced. You say it's strong, but you make me wonder if maybe I've turned hard. A stock car has to have a certain softness in the suspension or the tires break free of the track too easily. There has to be a give. You make me wonder if I have any give left in my suspension."

"So, what? You walked away from NASCAR three years ago and have focused solely on becoming the new Number One driver in the Secret Service?"

She shook her head. "Nothing else."

"Damn, woman. You need to get a life."

"I don't even know what that means."

Jim looked up and down the hall. Past midnight, it had the silence of a hotel—a well sound-insulated, luxury one. It was just the three of them, the burgundy carpet, and the sconce lighting of the flowered wallpaper. He'd always been more of a Holiday Inn Express kind of guy when he couldn't sleep in his rig.

"Jim?" Reese voice was a soft suggestion, barely audible in the long hall.

He looked at her, really looked at her. The sadness in her eyes would put Malcolm to shame—except with Reese he knew that it was neither a shame nor a genetic predisposition as it was with Malcolm. Today had taught him that it was completely against her nature to look that way.

He had no resistance. There wasn't even thought as he

reached out and pulled her against him. He'd had the good fortune to have hugged plenty of women over the years, but holding Reese was the first time he'd ever hugged steel. Even as she leaned into him, her back was ramrod straight. When her arms came up around his shoulders, he could feel the impossible power of a woman who worked out for an hour every morning *before* starting her day—she wasn't Pilates fit, she was United States Secret Service fit.

Unable to help himself, he buried his face in her luxuriant fall of hair as they held each other.

She didn't ease into him, slowly relaxing until their bodies were melded together.

Reese Carver broke in a single slide of lost traction. One moment the woman of steel. The next pressed so tightly against him that he wondered if he'd ever been really held by a woman before.

It didn't last but a moment, but she showed him a window to a whole new world he'd never imagined.

REESE STEPPED into her room and turned on the light as the door snicked shut behind her. It was a small room, made to feel bigger with a large mirror above the dresser and mini fridge.

She looked at herself and studied the woman there.

Was that really her?

Suits had defined her since she'd been a kid. Her father had given her a full-body racing suit just like his when she was eight and she'd worn it with pride. The kids at school had teased her, but she hadn't cared, not really. Because it had her name above her left breast and Carver Family Racing across the back. By the time she'd donned her own Nomex racing suit and climbed into a car, it had fit like a second skin.

Three years in the Secret Service had done the same. Open-collar button-down shirt, dark blue or gray suit, polished black rubber-soled shoes, current issue lapel pin identifying her as part of the Presidential Detail at a glance. She slipped out of her suit coat and revealed the nylon webbing of her shoulder holster to the mirror's eye. That and the FN Five-seveN sidearm were a part of her as well.

But for just a moment in the hallway, she'd been a woman in a man's arms.

Even after an entire day of putting up with her bullshit attitudes and weird silences, he'd still held her as if she wasn't the disaster area that she knew herself to be. It was when he'd buried his face in her hair that it had undone her. She'd always thought of her hair as a shield—herself on one side and all of the bullies, assholes, and even the lovers carefully kept on the other.

Jim had taken no advantage of her. He'd somehow seen that for even a single moment, she'd just needed to be held.

The woman in the mirror looked back at her in confusion. If he'd grabbed her ass, or anywhere else, she'd have known what to do with him. A hot steamy kiss from an undeniably handsome guy pressed back against a hotel room door, that too was familiar.

But to simply be held. As he'd done at the bar when she'd told him the story of her father. The first time she'd ever told anyone that story in full.

And when they'd kissed, when she'd finally let him slip fully through the shield of her hair, it had been like pounding into Turn One.

Coming off the downshift.

Feeding the power toward Turn Two with the tires glued

into the groove despite the g-force dragging her head sideways.

Not there yet, but feeling the anticipation of the upshift and hammer-down launch onto the backstretch.

Jim's kiss had been like a blast of nitromethane in a top-fuel dragster, firing off nerve endings she didn't even know she had. It was an adrenaline rush she hadn't felt since...

Her image scowled at her.

...since running one and two with her pop at the Charlotte Motor Speedway.

Yet when she'd tried to pull him into her room and find that high-octane finish, he'd refused.

"It's not that I don't want to, Reese," he'd looked right at her so there was no way to doubt his sincerity. "Don't know as I've ever wanted anything more. But as much as I'd enjoy tonight, I'm guessin' that you wouldn't be enjoying tomorrow morning much more than a cottontail rabbit on a highway—pissed off and feeling run over."

The fact that he was probably right didn't make her feel any better at the moment. Even as she tucked her sidearm under her pillow and undressed, she could still feel the suits that had defined her life.

How strange that some blind spot of Jim Fischer's didn't see her armor at all.

CHAPTER FOUR

The day had been just as brutal as Jim had expected. That he'd spent half of the short night thinking about Reese asleep just next door hadn't helped matters.

Since when did he turn down a beautiful woman, no matter how much pain she was in? Since never. He'd learned that letting a woman have a good cry on his shoulder made him into a shining knight. And the sorry-for-doing-that make-up sex afterward was typically awesome.

But Reese was made of different, sterner stuff. She was like the difference between his old Kenworth semi-tractor with its cozy sleeping compartment versus a HETS tractor that hauled Abrams main battle tanks through the heart of a war zone.

He would've liked to start the day with something more friendly, but they'd barely had time for hello.

Morning route briefing over donuts and hotel coffee—really good hotel coffee, but of little help after a short night.

They'd had only a few minutes alone together on the drive to the Downtown Manhattan heliport but conversation had been about timing and logistics. Then he'd spotted Malcolm happily curled up in the First Lady's seat. Thankfully, among the weapons, gas masks, and other paraphernalia, the vehicle was also stocked with Windex and paper towels. He shuffled into the back and spent the last part of the drive cleaning up dog hair.

"Thanks, buddy."

Malcolm, who'd slept at the bar, in the hallway, and across his legs, offered him a lazy yawn that was hard to resist. He waved Malcolm out of the seat and onto the Suburban's carpeted floor.

"*Not* with the sad doggie eyes," Jim told him. "You know that doesn't work on me."

Malcolm sighed and moved to the floor. Jim began cleaning the back seat.

Reese's sad eyes of last night had certainly been gone this morning. She was back to pure Secret Service driver. It was a sunny day in February and her dark glasses were firmly in place, hiding all of her thoughts.

The moment he'd stepped out of the vehicle and onto the pier at the heliport was the very last he saw of Reese all day except at a distance.

He and Malcolm cleared the heliport terminal building, bathrooms, and finally the L-shaped pier that stuck out into the East River.

Reese rolled the bronze Suburban out onto the pier and turned it around, ready to depart.

He saw her watching him through the driver's window, but he and Malcolm were done scanning and there was no reason to delay. Back through the terminal, he was climbing into an idling black Suburban when he saw the white-top helo fly in over Brooklyn. An NYPD fast patrol boat circled beyond the pier while a helicopter gunship hovered above on Overwatch.

He shut the door and was whisked off to the first site on the First Lady's itinerary.

Other dog teams had secured the store, but he and Malcolm did a final walk-through of their precise route—information so compartmented that even most of the agents and NYPD didn't know it. Loading dock, freight elevator Number Three reserved for their exclusive usage, up to dresses, then over to shoes. He barely saw the ladies themselves as his work was done before they'd actually arrived.

He and Reese managed to exchange smiles as he headed out and was whisked off to the next site.

During the Broadway show, he'd constantly patrolled the lobby and backstage. The show had pyrotechnics and though there were two agents hovering over the technician and his supply of flammables and small explosives, the scent triggered poor Malcolm so often that they'd had to go for a long walk around the block just to calm his nerves.

Once they'd done the initial patrol at the Rum House—the place wasn't going to have nearly as many business-class cokeheads for a while—he'd mostly hung by the door, idly chatting with the bartender who doubled as a bouncer. It was a prime spot, anyone entering the bar would have to walk past Malcolm's sensitive nose.

Through the front window, he could just see Reese in the Suburban pulled close up to the curb with the rest of the Motorcade. She remained in the driver's seat, ready to evacuate the party at a moment's notice.

Harvey Lieber had been right, the three leading women of the White House were absolutely stunning together. He could see Ms. Matthews' calm sophistication, Ms. Taylor's class, and Ms. Darlington's whimsical sense of fun as the three of them laughed together over a late night snack.

Detra—the head of the First Lady's detail—flirted with him briefly each time she passed by on patrol. It seemed to just be a piece of who she was.

Beat Belfour—the head of Ms. Matthews' detail—gave him one withering look that said she be glad to neuter him slowly with a dull blade if he screwed up in the slightest. He actually wouldn't put it past her.

But it wasn't any of them he was thinking of.

The reserved agent who had sat at the front corner table with him last night occupied his thoughts so thoroughly that he was glad Malcolm was the one watching the door because he was doing a lousy job of it.

REESE HAD ENJOYED WATCHING Malcolm and Jim doing their job throughout the day. Even at the end of it, the dog still had a bounce in his step and Jim still had a smile for her each time he passed by.

The First Lady's Motorcade was quite different from the President's. Thirty-five vehicles were reduced to five or six other than a police escort. They were seen as significantly less tempting targets for foreign attackers. Especially the current and former First Ladies, as both were immensely popular.

So she'd spent her day never more than three steps from her vehicle inside a highly secure area. Police and a Sweep Car led the way. Then her vehicle, with the head of the First Lady's Protection Detail sitting where Jim had been all yesterday.

The contrast was jarring. Special Agent Detra Willand was a voluble and cheery blonde. She maintained that attitude even as she scanned for bad guys before opening the door for the ladies to exit the vehicle. As they rolled along between sites,

Detra had filled her in on news items and gossip as readily as route protection details.

Jim had been comfortable with the long silences as they'd ridden together around Manhattan. Detra was almost never silent, and by the end of the day, Reese was exhausted. She liked Detra. The agent would be a great person to spend a night out on the town with. But after a day together...the silence was welcome.

By the end of the day, sitting outside the Rum House and watching through the bar's front window as Jim was so perfectly vigilant, Reese could really appreciate him. She knew now that no matter how casually he sat at the end of the bar closest to the door and chatted with anyone who came up to him, he wouldn't miss a single thing.

He hadn't even missed that she *would* have hated herself this morning if she'd dragged him into her bed last night.

But that was last night.

She'd now had a whole day to watch him at a distance and think about it.

As usual, Jim departed minutes before her Motorcade did, rushing back to make sure the hotel was still secure as everyone reassembled in the vehicles. Once set, they rushed after him: police, Sweep Cars, her bronze Suburban with the three laughing women, and Detra once more chatting at her side. In the rearview mirror rolled Halfback—the heavily armed black Suburban that carried the rest of the First Lady's Protection Detail, a press van, the Roadrunner communications vehicle, and a police car tail.

When she finally reached her room, she was thrown by the Do Not Disturb sign hanging from Jim's door handle. Had she misread everything about the last thirty-six hours?

She considered knocking anyway and demanding answers.

She considered pulling out her sidearm and shooting out the lock. Instead, she retreated to her room to fume in private.

Her foot crunched on a note on hotel stationary that had been slid under the door. In a heavy block print was a simple note: *Our rooms have a connecting door.*

Reese hadn't given the inner door any thought last night except as a possible avenue of attack. Jim clearly had.

Before she could second guess herself, she stepped over and unlocked it from her side. When she swung it open, she saw that Jim's was already opened a crack.

Moment of truth, Reese.

Jim Fischer wasn't some contest, some race she had to win. But he definitely made a hell of a door prize.

She nudged the door open a little wider. Malcolm looked up at her from where he sprawled across the foot of the king-sized bed and wagged his tail. In the background, she could hear Jim's shower running. Again, the door was cracked slightly open spilling the only light into the room. An invitation.

Reese had always been a morning-shower person. A fresh start to the day. Hot water, soap, green starting flag, go! Jim seemed to be more of a wash-off-the-day type, which always struck her as a little defeatist. Tonight perhaps she'd ignore that. But she'd only taken that single indecisive step into the room when the shower shut off.

She froze for a long moment while Malcolm watched to see what she'd do.

Never be here in the first place was most best option—hasty retreat and trust Malcolm to not give away her indecision. But now that she was here, retreating wasn't an option. The right solution? Pedal to the metal.

Reese stripped as she hurried to the far side of the bed. Jacket, blouse and slacks over a chair, shoes and underwear on the floor by the bed, sidearm under the pillow, she slipped between the covers. She wished she'd thought to swing the connecting door back into place.

She slipped down deeper in the covers and warmed her toes against Malcolm.

After another minute, Jim stepped from the bathroom. He was naked and backlit by the bathroom light. It made her catch her breath. He walked all day every day and his muscle definition, highlighted in the bright light, was incredible. Adding in workout shoulders and he was a vision sparkled by tiny drops of water.

Whether it was her sharp breath or his noticing the ajar connecting door, he spun to face the bed.

"Reese?"

She kept silent in the shadows, not sure if she could speak.

"Reese," her name turned thankful in his husky voice. It was enough to wash away her doubts. Though it wouldn't do to have him too assured of himself, not after the doubts he'd just put her through.

"Fischer," she kept it a simple acknowledgement she might use passing him in the hall of the West Wing.

She as much felt as heard his soft chuckle as he turned off the bathroom light. A dim nightlight in the bathroom spilled a soft glow into the room, just enough to track his movements. He crossed to the dresser first, where she heard a soft crinkle of foil.

"Pretty sure of yourself, buying condoms." And she didn't like that at all. Had he simply assumed that any woman would be glad to fall into his bed? It was almost enough to make her climb back out in the darkness.

"Part of Malcolm's med kit. If I have to bandage a bleeding paw fast, I won't have time to shave it before I tape it. Condom first, then tape over that so that I don't catch his fur."

"Oh," she pulled the half discarded sheet back into place. "Better not hurt a paw anytime soon," she warned the dog.

"Don't worry, I carry plenty."

"Were you a boy scout? Always prepared?"

"Eagle scout." He slipped in between the sheets and an exploring hand landed on the flat of her belly. "And not ready for you."

It was a corny line, except the way he said it, it didn't sound like a line at all.

Rather than sliding up to grope her breast, his hand continued around her waist, then hauled her against him as if she weighed nothing. He was even careful not to snag her long hair as he pulled them together.

No kiss, no grope. Instead, he pulled her into a hug as tight as last night's and held them together.

For a long moment, she could feel herself holding tension, like waiting for the starter's flag. In many ways it was the most adrenaline filled moment of the race—all anticipation and withheld action.

But Jim didn't start, instead he simply held her close.

As if he was waiting for something.

As if he was waiting for…her.

No man ever did that. Apparently Jim Fischer did.

She relaxed into him, sensations scorching along her skin as more and more of their bodies came into contact. Jim was warm from the shower and just a tantalizing bit cool from the sparkles of water that he'd missed toweling off. It made him feel more three dimensional. Like that moment she'd first run into his back in the West Wing—impossibly real.

He'd forgotten a razor when they'd stopped for essentials and she could feel his two-day beard as he buried his nose in the crook of her neck. Ignition sparks followed his hand as he brushed up to her shoulders, then slowly down her bare back and finally caressed her behind.

"*That,*" Jim whispered, "is an amazing ass."

Far too many men had said that in one form or another. She was black, not some ass-flat white chick. But she was so tired of men saying so.

Reese's arms were around Jim's back, so she couldn't punch him.

Instead she thumped a fist as hard as she could into his kidney.

PAIN ROCKETED up Jim's back. Not enough to make him scream as she had a lousy angle on him, but enough to engage a hundred percent of his attention. And to make him accidentally jam out his legs.

Malcolm responded with a yelp of surprise and a hard thump as he fell off the foot of the bed and onto the carpeted floor.

"Sorry, Malcolm," Reese whispered out into the darkened room.

"Sorry, Malcolm? He's not the one you just punched in the kidneys."

"He's also not the one who just told me I was hot because of the shape of my ass."

Jim groaned a bit as he tested his back with a careful twist. If that was a near miss, he couldn't imagine what a direct strike from Reese would feel like.

"Did I hurt you much?"

"Enough," he winced as he shifted.

"Good!"

Deciding that his fate was in his own hands, Jim reached under her arms and grabbed her behind again.

Because he kept his elbows out, her next swing bounced harmlessly off his ribs.

"This…" he squeezed her tightly so there was no question about what he was talking about.

She tried once more to thump him and growled at her inability to strike her target.

"…is a truly exceptional piece of anatomy on a beautiful woman. It also had nothing to do with why I'm in bed with you."

"Oh, but my breasts do?"

"Again, exceptional examples from what little experience I've had with them. Again, not particularly relevant."

"Okay, Fischer, why the hell are you in bed with me?"

"You mean other than it being my bed and you're the one who's in it, not the other way around?"

"Yes, other than that." He could hear her gritting her teeth and he liked doing that to her. A little payback for the kidney shot, a little bit keeping her off balance. He suspected that Reese was too used to a certain kind of man having a certain kind of expectation of this beautiful woman.

"Because from the first moment, you've been nothing like I expected."

She didn't even hesitate. "Because I didn't throw myself at you from the first moment?"

"Because you keep being so much more than I expect. Then I raise those expectations and you either blow right by them or go sideways around them."

"What did you expect?" She finally stopped any sign of struggling, but he wasn't going to let his guard down just yet.

"At first the wide-eyed newbie. But then Dilya liked you and that kid goes deep in ways I guess I'll never understand.

You take the hit of losing your father. The way that happened, you could have hung it up and shriveled away worse than corn in a drought—most folks would. Instead, you come back as the driver of Stagecoach. Damn, woman! Then you've got an ass that feels as good as this," he stroked it more gently this time and just couldn't believe how soft her skin was over all that smooth muscle. "Is there anything you can't do?"

"Apparently, understand an Okie."

"Good, maybe that will keep you around a while trying to figure me out. Because you've sure got this good ol' boy mystified."

"Let's see if I can demystify a thing or two."

CHAPTER FIVE

*N*ot only did Reese know that she had a fine ass, when she woke up the next morning, she felt it too. Jim hadn't focused on it alone. In fact, he'd gone to some impressive effort so that not a single inch of her felt neglected.

Clothes in her hand, she headed to her own shower so as not to wake him—the man had earned his sleep. Gods, had he earned it.

Reese felt loose, like a cat on the prowl. Curiously comfortable with her nakedness in a man's room like she'd never been. She'd always been the one to race to the finish, won and done. Always first dressed.

Jim had refused to be hurried. And it hadn't been just his hands or his mouth. He'd rubbed her instep with the top of his foot like he was performing reflexology on the pressure points there rather than just a nice contact. When she'd looped a leg over his hips, he'd taken the time to massage the calf muscles and reshape her until she lay more tightly against him than she'd thought physically possible.

She stood at the connecting door and looked back at him.

The predawn light leaking around the edges of the hotel curtains revealed him flat on his back and arms flung wide, like a man cut down in his prime. It made her smile. He somehow *knew* that she would want to be on top. No power games, no avoidance. He'd let her ride him and take control, the only way she'd ever found to reach that pinnacle of release. Yet Jim hadn't been merely compliant even then. Instead he'd teased, enhanced, driven her until she'd forgotten everything other than her own body and the man giving it all of his attention.

There really wasn't time this morning, but she wished she had a chance to see if he could take her to that same impossible place again.

That's when she spotted the butt of her handgun sticking out from under her pillow. She tiptoed back, circling wide around Malcolm, who lay on Jim's jeans and tracked her with only his eyes.

As she reached for her HK Five-seveN, a hand clamped around her wrist. It was startling. She hadn't slept with many white men, and the contrast of their skin was a surprise. Light and shadow. Whole and…Reese didn't know what she was, but definitely not whole.

Without a word, Jim slowly dragged her toward him. She should resist, she should protest. His grip was actually only tight enough to ease her toward him and would be nothing to break from. Instead she dropped her clothes. There was a muffled woof of surprise and then a quick rattle of his collar as Malcolm shook free of her clothes.

"Shh," Jim whispered to her. "Don't wake the kid."

"There isn't time."

"Hush. There's always time." And he pulled her in until she had no choice except to lie down against him, tucked inside the curl of his arms.

Resigned to the inevitable, not that she could really think of any reason to complain, she relaxed into him.

And he held her.

Nothing more.

Until she wondered if he had gone back to sleep.

She tried to raise up to look at him, but he rested his hand on her head and eased her back down onto his shoulder.

"Just lie still a moment. A man likes a moment to appreciate waking up beside a fine-assed woman."

In one night, he'd managed to turn a phrase that had made her livid as hell her whole life into a tease, almost an... endearment. He made it sound as if they had a deep and abiding relationship, not an absolutely incredible one-night stand. She was even less used to endearments than she was to lasting relationships.

As he continued to lie there, holding her close, she could almost believe in it though. She wasn't very skilled at relationships longer than one-night stands, because they required on-going civility. Or maybe because... Reese no longer knew. All she could think about was how nice it felt to lie here in a lover's arms and pretend nothing more existed.

"You know," Jim whispered softly.

"Yes?" Her voice was a smooth, liquid tone that she didn't recognize at all. It was the tone of a woman's voice in the movies before she made love to a man. Which sounded like a very good idea. She slid her hand down his stomach to see what his body's thoughts were on the subject.

"We're going to be incredibly late if you don't get that fine ass of yours moving right quick." Between one heartbeat and the next, Jim rolled out of her reach and she was watching *his* fine white ass as he strode for his bathroom.

She lay there for a long moment in disbelief, then rolled out herself and regathered her clothes and her sidearm.

"I'm sorry, Malcolm," she paused to rub the dog's belly with her toes. "But I'm going to have to kill your master. Just thought you should know."

Malcolm considered for a moment, then flopped onto his back so that she could keep rubbing his belly. She continued for a few more moments, then smirked at the half-open bathroom door as she headed for her own shower. If the man thought he was going to sway her choices and beat her that easily, he had another thought coming.

DAY THREE and Jim was done in. Even Malcolm was dragging and he never dragged.

It wasn't last night. He'd never woken up feeling so alive. He missed his first chance to keep Reese beside him because the woman went from asleep to full speed in about two seconds flat. He was a morning person too, but there were some limits.

But he'd had his chance when she came back for her sidearm. He found it there in the middle of the second round of the night's gymnastics. During the first he probably could have grabbed onto a hot exhaust manifold and not have noticed the burn—Reese felt that incredible.

When she slid back in beside him, he'd had his chance to imagine what it was like waking up next to Reese when she wasn't running off like a house afire. *Damned nice!* For all her hard edges and abrupt lane shifts, when she gave, she did it at full throttle as well—racing was definitely the right metaphor for Reese Carver. A breathtaking display of physical ability fueled by raw heat. Last night she'd seared his memories with her body until no one else's remained.

And this morning, when she strode across his hotel room

wearing nothing but a smile… Well, nobody got that lucky and he wasn't sure why she'd decided it would be him. It really was a pity that they'd run out of time and he'd had to yank himself away from her. He had rather hoped that she'd join him in the shower, but he knew some women preferred to do such things in private and he hadn't wanted to pressure her.

"We gotta find a way to keep her around," he told Malcolm.

The dog barely looked up at him. It was their last stop of the day and they'd done their duty. The Downtown Manhattan Heliport was fully secure. They'd patrolled from the front steel gates along FDR drive, throughout the small parking lot, inside and out of the terminal building, the narrow driveway along one side of the pier, and around the various helicopters waiting to whisk the protectees back from where they'd come.

"Now just the ride home, boy."

Malcolm sighed and plopped his butt on the sidewalk by the front gate to await the Motorcade already en route from the UN.

The lead route vehicle came by, slowing down only long enough to exchange a wave with the head of the detail waiting at the gate. That meant the rest of the Motorcade was less than a minute out. Jim spotted the flashing lights far down FDR well before he could hear the sirens. He and Malcolm were done except for the ride home.

"Looking forward to putting more fur on the First Lady's seat?"

Malcolm looked up at him. Absolutely.

"Looking forward to a four-hour ride back to DC with Reese Carver?" Jim asked himself.

That sounded mighty good as well. Maybe on the way back she'd stop at a store for Fritos and root beer. Still odd not being the driver. Except for trading shifts on the long-hauls— they'd often do four hours on/four hours off for the entire duration of the Kandahar run—he wasn't used to the passenger seat.

Felt as if he was doing that in many ways with Reese Carver, hanging on for dear life in more ways than one.

He could hear the sirens now.

"Hang in there, buddy."

He wasn't sure which of them he was talking to. Neither was Malcolm.

REESE LIKED that Jim had *not* asked why she didn't join him in the shower. It meant that he was deliberately messing with her head and the game was still on. She was down with that.

The New York trip was in the home stretch—the final drive from the UN back to the Marine's white-top helos waiting on the pier. The three women in the back were talking softly and even Detra in the right-hand seat was quiet. It had been a long couple of days for everybody and they'd all be ready to be done with it and get back to DC.

They emerged from the last tunnel two hundred yards from the heliport.

Up ahead she spotted a man and his dog leaning against the heavy steel corner post of the front gate. She'd give a lot to know what he was thinking. Which was a surprise. Normally she didn't give a damn. Actually, that wasn't right—normally she *knew*. Men were predictably interested in sex and power games. Yet even if Jim had been an enthusiastic lover, he'd been a very thoughtful and thorough one. He'd made sure it was about her as much as about him. Maybe he'd done that just to confuse her. If that was his intent, it had worked.

The six-motorcycle V was keeping the FDR's right lane clear. She followed the Lead Car closely, not liking the tightness of the space as they emerged from the tunnel, a tall concrete wall to her right slowly tapering down as the Motorcade climbed.

At a hundred yards out, they were just close enough to make out Malcolm's coloring, white-and-brown, but not yet close enough to separate out the small black police vest that also served as his harness.

That's when she spotted a flicker of movement off her left side.

Before she had even fully registered it, her NASCAR instincts had crashed her foot into the floor and had her heading right until she was nearly into the four-foot vertical wall that separated the highway from a parallel lane of merging traffic. The Suburban's big V-8 engine roared to life and they accelerated sharply.

Detra started some question from the passenger seat, which Reese ignored.

She barely had time to see the massive grillwork on the twenty-four-foot delivery truck arrowing in on her before it clipped her back end.

For half a second, terror slammed into her as her rear tires broke traction and went sideways. She bounced the right rear fender off the concrete wall. They'd have been pinned, perhaps crushed, but she reached the end of the barrier and was able to swing into the open merging lane. If she hadn't accelerated when she did, the truck would have rammed squarely into her door.

There were screams from the women in the back—high and panicked, like the screams of her father's tires as they broke free on the Charlotte Motor Speedway.

Then Reese recovered. They weren't going two hundred miles an hour, out at the performance limits of a racing stock car. This was a big, tough, four-wheel drive Suburban doing its best to climb from sixty to seventy miles an hour. She snapped the steering wheel right, then left to regain control.

The black BMW Lead Car that had been immediately in front of her veered into the left lane to clear a path for her, then the driver slammed on his brakes—smoking his tires.

In her side mirror, Reese could see the BMW take the blow. The big delivery truck plowed into the rear of the BMW—forty thousand pounds versus four thousand. That Secret Service driver had just bought himself a long stay in the hospital and her eternal thanks.

The rear of the BMW disappeared in a cloud of debris before the car was flipped up and over backward. It buried its nose through the truck's windshield.

Lurching to one side, the truck caught a wheel and tipped over, skidding along the road, throwing showers of sparks in every direction. The passenger compartment of the BMW was battered aside and spun into oncoming traffic causing a chain reaction of swerving cars, squealing brakes, and crunching metal.

Reese kept her foot in it as they crossed eighty miles an hour.

Congestion ahead—the police leading the Motorcade no longer clearing the path but rather blocking it as they slowed in surprise. She jumped the curb separating traffic from a two-way paved bicycle lane. She barely missed taking out two cyclists and a line of park benches along the sidewalk. With a sharp swerve, then a counter, she was able to avoid the cyclists, then the fire hydrant on the divider.

In a final glance back, Reese could see that Halfback—the heavily armed Suburban that had been on her tail—was also tangled up in the mess and now lay flipped onto its roof. Despite that, agents with MP5s and AR-15s were already out of their vehicle and surrounding the truck. At their lead was the fierce black woman who led former First Lady Matthews' detail. Her jacket was shredded and she was limping badly, but her weapon was out as she led the way.

Focus ahead.

The police motorcycles, unable to jump the curb, remained on the main lane of the FDR as Reese raced past them to the heliport's entry along the bike path. At the main gate, guards had their weapons up and one was waving her through.

Estimating the traction and the limits of the heavy Suburban, she waited as long as she dared.

Then she stood hard on the brakes to dump half her speed. At eighty, they'd just roll over for what she was planning.

Detra was shouting over the radio to have the helos ready. Not Reese's concern.

When the speedometer hit forty, Reese turned hard to the right, slapped the transmission down into second, and punched the gas.

The rear wheels broke free.

She counter-steered into the sliding drift, watching the big heavy stanchion on the far side of the main gate looming large and heading squarely at her own door. If she hit it too hard, there was nothing to stop her from plowing through it and dumping them all into the East River.

Holding the line, she suffered only a glancing blow that served to finish the drift.

Now headed down the pier at ninety degrees to where she'd been a moment before, she punched the gas, barely dodging around a hot dog vendor's cart. Down to thirty miles an hour but still in second gear gave her plenty of power when she goosed the engine.

A glimpse of Jim in the main parking lot, yelling toward the gate alongside the terminal that separated the parking lot from the narrow driveway onto the pier. They got it open just in time for her to barrel through without having to drive into it and risk hurting someone as she blew the inner gate off its hinges. The driveway between the terminal building and the edge of the pier was meant to be taken at five miles an hour—she didn't ease off the gas until she was nearing the helos.

One last time, she cranked the wheel and stomped down on the parking brake. The big Suburban went into a sideways slide along the pier toward the waiting Sikorsky White Hawk. She stopped under the edge of the spinning rotor disk—with a low dip of seven-foot-seven, her six-foot-two Suburban was clear. It might have given the pilot a heart attack, but Reese had trained on this. She'd managed to place herself so that the rear passenger doors of the Suburban were facing the helicopter's side door from less than ten feet away and any attack from the street would be shielded by the bulk of the Suburban.

Detra was gone out the passenger door and Reese could hear the women being unloaded from the rear and rushed unceremoniously into the waiting helo.

But all Reese could see was Jim and Malcolm racing down the pier toward her. He had his sidearm out—double-handed and aimed at the ground—and was swinging his head side-to-side watching for any renewed attack, but he was headed straight for her.

She didn't know if she'd ever seen such a welcome sight.

CHAPTER SIX

*U*nknown.

By the end of the day, Jim wanted to beat anyone who said that word.

"Unknown" had been the conclusion of everything. Was the truck driver a solo actor? A terrorist? A psycho? Or had he merely fallen asleep at the wheel? The BMW Sweep Car's driver and his right-seat fellow agent had busted up ribs and arms but had survived. There wasn't enough of the truck driver left to identify. First, his head and torso had been shattered by the nose of the BMW ramming through the windshield, then a fire had broken out. The spilled gas from the broken BMW finally found an ignition spark as the First Lady's helo lifted well clear and headed to JFK to meet the waiting Air Force jet.

The man who owned the truck had reported it stolen thirty-six hours earlier and had been found in a bar next door to his shipping business, enjoying a pint and a roast beef sandwich. He, for sure, hadn't enjoyed the rest of his night. His original load of fifteen thousand pounds of exercise equipment for a new gym had still been aboard but was a complete write-off. Despite his apparent innocence, he and his company would be on a terror watchlist for a long time to come.

Another group of agents were scanning traffic cameras hoping for a clear shot of the driver's face, but with little luck.

Other than battered metal, the Suburban had come through unscathed. He, Reese, and every other agent who'd been on the scene spent the entire night in the New York Secret Service office in Brooklyn going through every step of the thirty-seven seconds from the moment the truck had veered across FDR drive until the Sikorsky White Hawk had lifted its wheels off the pier.

When finally released, he and Reese had collapsed into a bed together, with Malcolm—the only one who'd slept that night—sprawled happily at their feet. Jim had held her close as she once more recounted each action, each motion, every nuance of what she'd done and felt.

"For just an instant, when everything broke loose, I saw my father. Saw his car right there in front of me. Except this time there was no helmet hiding his face. It was as if he was trying to say something, but I couldn't hear it."

She doodled a finger on his chest.

He'd seen it all unfolding.

The big truck swinging wide ever so briefly, as if gathering momentum for its slash across the lanes of the FDR. Or perhaps to get away from the rushing phalanx of the Motorcade's sirens and lights. A moment of inattention, bouncing a tire off the low divider between directions of the FDR, then overcorrecting? There was no way to be sure.

Reese sliding free after banging off the wall and the Lead Car braking to take the hit.

Jim had known what Reese would do—had known what he'd have done in the circumstances—but didn't get to see it.

He'd had to trust in her abilities as he turned to search for, and clear, anything that might slow her down.

The guards manning the inner gates were listening intently to their radios, unaware that five tons of armored SUV would be racing down on them in mere seconds. Unwilling to clutter the command frequency, he raced from the main gate toward the team manning the gate out to the pier. A quick hand signal had Malcolm following in a tight heel position, but on his right side, away from Reese's path.

He'd signaled and yelled for the agents to open the inner gate. They'd made it in time for Reese to race through.

He had ducked through himself moments before they slammed it shut and raised their weapons.

"Defend," he'd shouted, though they already were, and raced after Reese.

He'd almost choked as she slid the Suburban sideways beneath the spinning rotors of the helicopter. It was one of the slickest moves he'd ever seen...until last night when he'd watched the video of her passage through the main gate at speed.

"My dad," he told Reese as he held her in the dark until she finally wound down, "said that you're a crappy driver until you've driven your first hundred thousand miles. I didn't believe him, of course, until I had. Then I understood what he meant. I'd finally laid down enough miles to notice anything that *wasn't* normal. I've logged over a million now, and there's no way in hell I could do what you just did."

He could feel her shrug.

Everyone had been as impressed as hell when they'd seen the video, judging each slide so perfectly in an unfamiliar vehicle. She'd probably shaved five, maybe ten seconds off what any other driver could have done. But each time someone had commented on it, she'd shrugged it off.

"I wasn't the impressive one. It was the Lead Car driver who really did something, putting his life on the line without hesitation. All I did was drive."

"All you did was drive? You had one job, he had another. Even the very best drivers say they couldn't have done better; why aren't you letting that in?"

Again the shrug.

REESE LAY AWAKE a long time after Jim fell asleep.

He'd let her replay every instant of the incident until she was sure she wouldn't have done much different with a month's practice and planning.

Some way to prevent the necessity for the Lead Car driver's heroic act? None that she could think of.

Should she have worried about the truck in the other lane as they emerged from the tunnel? There was nothing to indicate that she should have.

Any race you finish alive is a good one. Any you complete with your car still running is a victory. How many times had Pop said that to her and her brother? But her brother had broken Pop's first rule shortly after Pop had.

He'd taken to racing motorcycles at a young age, and died attempting to jump a small ditch during the Dakar Rally in Argentina. A negligent moment—just five days after Pop died —not enough lift or maybe a crumbling edge…and he'd been flung headfirst into a tree. At least the death had been instantaneous. Pop had stayed conscious long enough for the ambulance to arrive, but hadn't even made it off the track.

By Pop's standard, she'd had a victory. By any standard.

Jim's final question rankled at her. So why *couldn't* she let it in?

CHAPTER SEVEN

*B*ack in DC, things fell quickly into routine—Jim's *old* routine.

With the intensity and intimacy of New York behind them, there was a distance in the present. Reese was the "golden one" from the moment they'd reentered Secret Service headquarters in DC. Lauded by everyone, he could see it eating at her. She disappeared in more ways than one.

She hadn't answered her cell phone when he tried it.

His text asking if she wanted to catch dinner—which he'd thought was fairly harmless—had received a two-word reply: *Need time.*

Now, a week later, Jim couldn't decide if he was as feeble as a glue horse for not pursuing her when she'd first tried to shut him out. What guy on the planet wanted to face the definitive "no" from a woman? "No" sucked. He had certainly received his share of "so long," "thanks," or that lamest of all "whatever" over the years. But not from the most incredible woman he'd ever been with.

He should have known something was wrong when he'd

woken up that next morning. She'd already been up and dressed. No friendly teasing her back into bed. No quick snuggle to mark the start of a new day. It was still the old day—they'd gone to sleep about dawn after the long debriefing and it was just after lunchtime when they woke—so he figured that was fair, if regrettable.

"It's two o'clock and I'd like to get on the move before rush hour," Reese had told him as she finished fastening her shoulder harness.

Which he supposed was reasonable enough. The Suburban had only suffered cosmetic damage, so the two of them drove it back to DC for repairs.

No fresh news when they'd checked in, so the drive south had been mostly quiet, just watching the changes of the day as it rolled through evening and into night. He'd asked her a bit about racing, he'd told her some exotic stories of driving big rigs across the Afghan countryside, but for the most part they'd just fallen into the driver's rhythm of letting the road roll by.

Or so he'd thought. Until Reese Carver had evaporated.

He tried switching to a morning workout, but Malcolm didn't like the change-up in routine. After three days of not spotting her, he slid back into an after-shift workout.

Training Day came up on his duty roster.

It had been eight weeks and it was time for a refresher course for him and Malcolm out at RTC.

"Time to expose his nose to the stuff that explodes," as the course master Lieutenant Jurgen liked to say.

RTC was short for the James J. Rowley Training Center, the Secret Services' training grounds. Here they could attack helicopters and aircraft, drive militarized ATVs in the dirt, spin cars through twisted courses, and raid storefronts or skyscrapers. Almost every essential skill could be worked on here. The K-9 Training Center was a small corner of the complex. It contained an agility course and a mocked-up office building interior. For area work, there was a two-street town set up in a different section of RTC.

Tommy Jurgen was a tough sumbitch retired Marine and fellow Okie, so they got along just fine.

"So tell me," Jurgen didn't even let him get through the door of his office. No question what he wanted to know—Jim had been asked to tell the story all week.

So, he cracked a cold orange juice, tossed Malcolm a treat, and sat down to tell the tale of the most threatening attack on a Secret Service protectee in recent history. The newspapers had had a heyday of it, arguing both sides against the middle without the USSS saying a word: *US Secret Service saves the day,* and *First Lady nearly killed due to Secret Service negligence to detect the threat.*

The problem was that after a full week, there were still no leads on the truck's driver. Street cam footage had been pieced together over the entire thirty-six hours between the theft of the truck and the attack—and not one usable image of his face had been caught. They weren't even sure it was a he until the DNA analysis of the few teeth and bones that had been recovered. Beyond that, he was melting-pot American with no clear genetic history. Missing persons reports were being chased, but so far without any luck.

"Seems pretty unlikely for him to remain a John Doe for a full week," Jurgen scowled down at his boots. "Less'n he was tryin'."

"Yep," that had been everyone's conclusion. Jim told him the general consensus. "Deliberate attack by party or parties unknown. Assume significantly increased threat levels."

Jurgen scowled at the ceiling now as if searching for a different answer, but finally concluded, "Yep."

"Got another question for you." Jim knew he was fishing, but couldn't help himself.

"Fire away."

"You ever meet a Special Agent Reese Carver? Driver?"

Jurgen's smile grew quickly, in a way that had earned him the nickname Jerk Jurgen from all of the female officers. "Oh yeah. Majorly hot chick on the Presidential Detail. What about her?" Then he narrowed his eyes at Jim for a long moment. "No way! You?"

"I shouldn't have asked." Jim should have guessed at Jurgen's reaction. And it wasn't like Jim wanted that fact out in public, but he was absolutely desperate for any clues.

"Not a man in the Service hasn't looked at that piece of ass and wanted it," Jurgen was on a roll.

For the first time, Tommy Jurgen's attitude toward women rankled.

Jurgen finally caught a clue and harrumphed himself back into being human. "Word is that no one, and I mean *no one*, gets much more than a hello out before she shoots them down outta the sky. Looked her up once. All set to be the top chick NASCAR driver, better than Danica Patrick, until her daddy and brother ate it in the same week. Had to be tough. Made her hard."

No, Jim decided. Not hard exactly. There'd been nothing hard about the woman in his bed. Cautious. Which meant… what? He didn't really know.

But Jurgen was expecting some reaction. Jim shouldn't have said anything in the first place, but he had. Now all he could do was try to make sure there was no reason for Jurgen to spread the story. So he offered his best nonchalant shrug and a "Huh," of defeat.

"So, she put another guy in the dust. Just another in a long list, buddy," Jurgen took the bait. "Time to stop thinking about women. You and Malcolm ready? I've got the course set."

"We were born ready. Right, Malcolm?"

The springer spaniel wagged his tail, clearly tired of all the talk.

An entire office complex had been built above the dog kennels within an innocuous-looking barn at the edge of the RTC campus. It would be spiked with dozens of different explosive compounds to be found by the team and keep them sharp.

As to not thinking about women, at least one woman, Jim didn't see that happening any more than him becoming a Nebraska Cornhuskers' fan after being bred-and-buttered on the Oklahoma Sooners. Nope, this trucker boy wasn't ready to give up on Reese one little bit.

"Let's do it." He slapped his knees as he rose and Malcolm jumped up ready to catch the bad guys, even if they were just pretend ones...today.

"SOMETHING EATING AT YOU?" Harvey Lieber had walked up to the desk Reese was using without her even noticing. When she'd glanced back during the attack, Reese had the best angle on the truck driver, but all she remembered was the truck's grill. She was flipping through the mug shot books on the chance that something would jog her memory, but so far no joy.

"No, sir. Just wishing I'd looked more carefully."

"Looked carefully enough to save your protectees. We're giving you the Director's Award of Valor for that."

"Don't want it, sir. I wasn't brave. Or *not* brave. I just drove. The two guys in the Lead Car—that was bravery."

"Yeah well, all three of you are getting one, so deal with it. Distinguished Service Award to your pal Fischer for fast thinking, too. Thinking of pulling him off Baxter's fence line detail and adding him to the Presidential team. What's your assessment?"

Reese wanted to say no, but knew that wasn't right. She remembered him racing to clear her way to the helos. On the camera footage, she'd seen him reacting several seconds ahead of any other agent—she'd still been bouncing off the wall and he'd already seen that she'd need a clear path. In NASCAR, races sometimes came down to thousandths of a second, making Jim's reaction time really stand out.

"He's a good man," was the very least he deserved.

Harvey Lieber narrowed his eyes at her for several long seconds, but she wasn't going to reveal anything else. He finally nodded to himself and turned away, making some inscrutable decision that she'd only find out about later.

"Are you two up to the Meryton Hall dance, or the Netherfield ball?"

Reese twisted around the other way to discover that Dilya and Zackie the First Dog had come up on her other side. She had the distinct impression that they'd somehow come to be there without Harvey even noticing. Dilya was dressed in form-fitting black—t-shirt, leggings, tennis shoes as dark as her hair—except for the bright rainbow-colored shoelaces woven between the eyelets in some strange and intricate pattern. Maybe this was her stealth mode.

"I don't know what you're talking about."

"You don't know *Pride and Prejudice*," Dilya shook her head with sadness. "I'm reading her other books now. I like Fanny in *Mansfield Park*, but that's because she's sort of like me, not like you."

"Whereas I'm like..."

"Elizabeth Bennet."

Reese wondered if all conversations with Dilya were like this. "You'd have to ask Jim about the story, I don't know it."

"Oh, I can tell you, if you'd like, but it might spoil the fun."

"The fun." What part of any of this was being fun?

Dilya nodded happily, then thought for a moment. "I know what you need. You need to go for a walk. Too bad there aren't any rain-muddied meadows. C'mon." And she turned for the Ready Room's door without waiting to see if Reese followed.

At the moment, anything was better than staring at thousands of pictures in hopes of spotting someone she'd never actually seen.

Dilya had turned right out of the Secret Service Ready Room, but she didn't go up the stairs—which was a huge relief. Up those stairs was the First Floor of the West Wing, including the Oval Office. If Reese *never* went up those stairs, it would be fine with her.

Instead, Dilya lead her back through a warren of offices and through a small door that she needed her security badge to unlock.

"Where—"

"Shh!" Dilya held a finger to her lips, then whispered, "There's a press conference going on, I don't want them to hear us. But this way is shorter."

The low-ceilinged area was filled with racks of equipment. Stacks and stacks of computers, high-speed modems, and video processors stood in long rows. Despite the soft roar of fans, the area was warm with radiated heat. She saw labels on the racks: ABC, NBC, CNN... She looked up at the ceiling when a sudden roar of voices sounded above. They were directly under the Press Briefing Room and the gaggle was shouting out questions for the Press Secretary.

They were in FDR's old swimming pool—in the deep end.

She looked at a small section of exposed wall and spotted the old tile that had originally walled in the pool. It was now covered with signatures of the press corps. FDR had swum here. JFK and Marilyn Monroe had probably frolicked together in this very spot. What were they...

Dilya had moved down to the far end of the pool. Zackie's nails clicked on the bare concrete floor that had replaced the old pool bottom.

Reese hurried along the cramped aisle to join her.

"This door leads into the Press Corps basement offices, but they should be empty right now." Dilya opened the door and led the way.

Down one side was a long line of tiny booths set up like the announcer's broadcast studios at NASCAR races. The door plaques showed that's exactly what they were: Voice of America, American Forces Network, Reuters, and more. On the left was a cubicle row, crowded aisles of small desks with cameras and notepads scattered about. There was a small rail with dozens and dozens of overlapping neckties dangling from it. Reese had no time for anything more than impressions as Dilya hurried along.

At one of the cubicle desks, a reporter hunched over a camera. Perhaps because the camera was broken there was no point in being upstairs at the briefing. All she could really see as they hurried by was the reporter's hands working on it. Close by lay a stack of several black boxes, each smaller than a pack of playing cards that must be some form of storage or battery she wasn't familiar with.

They passed a stairwell leading upward from which she could hear the clear voices of the press briefing breaking up. She raced ahead.

Past a tiny kitchen with two vending machines, a microwave, and an espresso machine with a picture of Tom

Hanks above it, they came to another door. Again, Dilya slotted her ID and a flat panel at the end of the hall swung aside. Zackie pushed through first.

They rushed through after her as steps sounded on the stairs from the offices above. Dilya leaned on the panel and it snicked shut with seconds to spare. The sudden silence was echoing.

They were in a utilitarian hallway that Reese's sense of direction said was a basement beneath the White House Residence itself. There was the rattle of dishes and the hum of a dishwasher off to her left. To the right was a long wall with two doors, both labeled Storage.

Directly in front of them, in the middle of a long white hallway lit fluorescent white, stood a gray-haired woman. Her hair was back in a bun. She wore an unremarkable dress and a knit red cardigan. She looked like someone's grandmother, if not for her brilliant blue eyes that were watching the two of them closely.

"Miss Stevenson," the woman nodded to Dilya. "We meet at long last. And Miss Carver. This is indeed a treat. And where are the two of you headed in such a hurry?"

Reese opened her mouth, then closed it again. She didn't know. Now that she thought about it, she was simply glad that no one was about to shoot her for trespassing where mere Motorcade drivers were *not* meant to go. Yet she had the distinct impression that this woman had been standing here waiting just for them.

"Uh..." It was nice to see the supremely confident Dilya flummoxed by something. The young know-it-all had clearly been having fun messing with her. Turnabout was such sweet revenge.

"You may call me Miss Watson. Where were you off to, child?" The woman didn't offer to shake hands, instead keeping them clasped on the carved white handle of her stout wooden cane. It looked as ancient as she did.

"I was taking Ms. Carver to go and see Clive." Dilya's tone said that she was distinctly unhappy about the "child" comment, but wasn't comfortable arguing with an elder—at least not one as imposing as Miss Watson.

Their destination was news to Reese. Clive who?

"Of course you were, dear. And I know for exactly what reason. How convenient that he has just made me a small delivery this morning. Please, come to my office." Again without waiting for any acknowledgement, she turned toward the sound of the dishwashing.

A few steps along the hallway, Miss Watson opened a door onto a narrow spiral stairway. Firmly grasping the handrail, the woman navigated the spiral downward with surprising agility. When Dilya followed, Reese was left with no choice but to do the same. They emerged into an even more utilitarian hallway of the subbasement. Excess chairs, perhaps from the State Dining room, were stacked along one side of the hall. Fold-up tables could be seen further along. Doors were labeled Air Conditioning, Storage, Dentist—with no dentist at present —Elevator Machinery, and finally Mechanical Room 043.

Miss Watson unlocked the door to that last and slipped inside.

At first impression, it looked like a dark hole. The kind that people entered, then were never seen again. A dim desk lamp was turned on, revealing a battered steel desk and shelves of books.

"If you'd give an old lady a hand, my dear," Miss Watson waved at the joint of two bookcases—after the brightness of the hall it was too dim to read any of the titles.

In for a penny. Reese took in a breath and, hoping that she would still be alive to take in another, pushed. The two bookcases swung inward and apart, sliding easily out of the way.

A parlor, brightly lit with Tiffany lamps, was revealed. It had a white oriental rug, delicate armchairs, and walnut fixtures. Miss Watson shuffled past, and at the touch of a switch, a gas fireplace flickered to life beneath a large marble mantel that might have dated all the way back to George Washington. There were pictures of women's faces everywhere. The room was elegant. And easily the most unexpected place she'd ever been.

Dilya's wide-eyed expression said this was new to her as well.

Miss Watson crossed to a bright red ceramic Snoopy doghouse. Lifting the dog as a handle, she removed the roof and revealed a cookie jar filled with dog biscuits. She selected one and bent down far enough to hand it to Zackie, then pat her on the head.

"Please," she waved them to chairs while she busied herself with a white porcelain teapot covered in sweet peas.

Reese looked once more at the photos about the walls. They came from every era of the nation's history, some were hand-painted portraits, but most were photographs. She identified Spanish, Russian, German, and Vietnamese women as well as a wide variety of ones in American military attire.

"Yes," Miss Watson spoke without turning. "Many of the finest spies throughout history have been women." As if she already knew what question Reese was thinking.

She delivered teacups and small plates of delicate chocolates before sitting in a flowered chair across from them. Perhaps this Clive was the White House chocolatier. She knew he worked somewhere in the lower reaches of the Residence, though she hadn't been aware that the building went this far down.

"Tell me what you know but haven't spoken aloud, Miss Carver." She propped her antique cane beside her chair and picked up her teacup.

There was something odd about the cane. It had tarnished metal on the tip and rose in a long taper, wider at the top than the tip by at least an inch. The carved handle looked like old deer horn, handled so often that it had been burnished smooth. Rather than having a flat top to rest one's palm on, as an invalid's cane might, it curved slightly. More like a handle if one were to hold it horizontally.

"Yes, an elegant piece," Miss Watson didn't even glance toward it.

She had a disconcerting way of never looking at what she was discussing.

"Jim Bowie was nearly killed by this sword cane during a duel on a sandbar in the Mississippi. Instead, he killed the man who stabbed him in the chest with it. It was because of that fight that he purchased a large knife from a blacksmith—a knife that was popularized as the Bowie knife. The knife came after the fight, despite the popular story. He also was a spy for the Americans against the Mexicans before he was ultimately killed at the Alamo."

"Can I see?" Dilya set down her cup.

"*May* I see. And yes." At Miss Watson's nod, Dilya stepped forward and picked up the cane.

"Just tug sharply, dear."

Dilya yanked on the handle and a foot and a half of bright steel slid out of the scabbard. It caught the red light off the Tiffany lamps until it looked as if it dripped with blood.

Miss Watson offered her pointers on how to hold and wield a sword. As Dilya practiced them, Reese noticed that Miss Watson's attention was on her, not Dilya.

Tell me what you know but haven't spoken aloud, Miss Carver.

Reese swallowed hard. Now it felt as if Miss Watson was a telepath placing her words directly into Reese's head.

She knew that she missed Jim Fischer and Malcolm. She shouldn't—not for how briefly they'd been together—yet she did. It was impossible that this unknown woman would be discussing that.

Therefore the topic, as it had tediously been all week, was the attack on the First Lady's Motorcade. Others were still debating between accident and attack, but she knew it was the latter. She also knew…but that was ridiculous.

Miss Watson smiled. "Yes, we *know* things even though there is no way for us to know them. That is the power of being a woman. You must learn to trust your instincts in life just as you did on the track. Tell me about the attack."

"I don't know your clearance."

"I should think that these walls speak for themselves," Miss Watson waved her teacup in a small circular motion that included far more than the unusual parlor in the deep subbasement that she occupied, perhaps even more than the White House itself. "But I don't care for such trivial items as what occurred. I already know all of that. I'm far more interested in what *you* know, but that others have not yet been willing to confront."

"It was a test." Reese hadn't known that for a fact until she said it aloud. But now that she'd given it a voice, she knew it was true.

"Oh my," Miss Watson stared down at her tea with pursed lips. "I had feared as much."

"A test of what?" Dilya paused halfway through a lunge with the blade.

"Of…" Reese didn't like the answer on the tip of her tongue. "Of Motorcade security. I have to tell Harvey. We have to lock it down harder." The realization slammed into her like a physical blow. She was halfway to her feet when Miss Watson held up a restraining hand. "What?"

"There is a question that you haven't asked yet, but which any of these women now hanging as memories on my wall would think of immediately."

Reese sat back and thought hard about what that might be. She even gave herself some time by eating the first chocolate. The deep flavors of strawberry and mint on a dark chocolate substrate almost served to distract her.

Almost.

"There is a hard-learned lesson by women of…" Miss Watson looked momentarily uncomfortable, "…my profession. Sometimes, an enemy's action is done to better understand our *reaction*."

Reese thought of racing, and it made perfect sense. There were times when you teased at a move, perhaps a couple times without executing it, to set up an opponent to be too slow to react when you finally did drop a gear to jump down to the inside of the track and take the lead from them. She'd done just that several times, but with a stock car. To do it with a Presidential Motorcade…

"But what did they learn?" Dilya slid the sword back into its cane scabbard and scooped up her third chocolate.

"That's the question, isn't it?" Miss Watson looked directly at Reese as if she knew the answer.

Dilya also looked at her for a long moment, then her eyes widened as if she too knew the answer.

Well *she* certainly didn't know it herself. The only thing they would have learned was…about Reese's driving. She was the latest unknown factor to be added to the Presidential Motorcade. Had they been trying to test her…or remove her?

She'd suddenly lost her taste for chocolate.

MALCOLM HAD DONE his typical stellar job on the training course. His sniffing score was at the top of the charts, and for a medium-sized dog, he'd done incredibly well on the agility course. For an hour he'd jumped over barriers, ducked and run through winding tunnels of plastic pipe, slalomed through stick gates like legs of fifty people in a crowd—all around proving that at four years old he was still a young dog in top form. Another half hour of attack training. Just because he was a "friendly" dog meant to be working among the public didn't mean he couldn't be dangerous when needed. Then a second run at an altered explosives course while they were both tired.

"I sometimes suspect your dog of cheating," Jurgen grumped as he signed off on the score sheet.

Jim looked down at his springer spaniel.

Malcolm gave back his best innocent look as if he knew exactly what they were talking about.

"Did you place all the explosives yourself?" Jim took a guess.

"Damn straight!"

"Wearing gloves?" Jim smiled.

Jurgen scowled down at Malcolm for a long couple seconds, then cursed when he figured out the drift of Jim's question.

"You little, four-legged sneak."

Jim burst out laughing. "Malcolm did a double find. He went after the explosives. And for the ones that were hardest to find, he went after the scent that the earlier ones had in common: you."

"That'll teach me." Jurgen offered a hard laugh, then thumped Malcolm on the ribs a few times to show that there were no hard feelings.

With his high scores, Malcolm had earned them an afternoon off.

Jim thought about hanging around until he saw what was next on Jurgen's agenda when a truck rolled up with a fresh load of ten dogs from Vonn Liche Kennels. Ten dogs tagged as candidates for the Secret Service's intense standards. He'd thought it could be fun, until he saw that they were all for the ERT.

The Emergency Response Team dogs were the toughest animals in the service: Dobermans, German shepherds, and Belgian Malinois. Driven, dangerous, and, after the long drive from Indiana, they would be a particular handful.

With thinly veiled excuses, which Jurgen saw right through but let him get away with, Jim and Malcolm made good their escape and climbed back into his pickup to head out.

The kennels and the bulk of the dog training area were in the farthest corner of RTC. Then there was the mock town, an area of tightly convoluted back roads for driver training, and then the main driving area for skid and turn training. The last was an open area of pavement a quarter mile long and a football field wide. If no one else was running, maybe they'd let him sign out a vehicle. Watching Reese on the videos, he'd learned more than a few tricks and wanted to give them a try. His job was no longer behind the wheel, but that didn't stop him from wanting to do it on occasion.

He pulled up beside the long line of battered Suburbans, Chevy Impalas, and Ford Tauruses that were used for agent's driver training. Once they were retired from the field, they were used and abused here. After they were truly worn out, they were repurposed once more for demolition derby training. *That* was a skill he was fine without learning—how to use another vehicle to bounce off for a change of direction or to shove into an assailant's path. Jim just wanted to try that high-speed drift.

Even as he opened his truck's door, he could hear the hard squeal of tires as someone worked the pavement on the other side of the garage. He rolled down the windows halfway and left Malcolm asleep on the front passenger seat. He'd earned his rest and the cool February day wouldn't bother him any. Jim tossed a light blanket over him anyway so that just his nose was sticking out.

After shrugging on his sheepskin jacket against the cool day, he walked around the end of the garage. Three guys were standing on the swatch of brown grass that separated the back of the main garage from the open stretch of pavement. They weren't doing anything, just watching.

Focusing downfield, he saw only one car on the big open area. It was one of the Beast limousines. The Presidential Motorcade only used three limos at a time: the President's and the two Spares. But the Secret Service actually owned twelve. Some were for backups when one or another was rotated into service. Others were for this.

The lone driver raced the car straight at them from the far end. With less than two hundred feet to go, the car slammed sideways into a four-wheel drift.

Before it even came to a stop, the rear tires smoked in reverse. With a hard cut, the driver was headed back the way they'd come, back end first. He could hear the engine clawing up against redline before the driver threw in the inevitable J-turn. A hard crank of the wheel. Rather than holding the sideways skid, they let the car drift around until it was headed nose-first down the field and the engine was gunning ahead in drive with almost no loss of speed despite the flip.

Jim strode up beside the guys watching. He'd expected to see Ralph McKenna out there taking one last set of spins before retirement, but instead he was standing here with the two head trainers. They all stood with their arms folded over their chests, just watching.

"Hey, guys."

"Hey, Jim," Ralph was the only one who glanced away from the driver long enough to identify him.

"Thought that'd be *you* out there."

"Technique's wrong," Arturo, the head trainer observed. "Ralph always hit the turn at five thousand RPM."

"That was fifty-five if it was a day," George, his assistant, added in.

"It was six flat. Hard against the redline," McKenna finished the conversation.

"Who..." But then he saw it. He'd watched the video a hundred times of Reese sliding the Suburban sideways at high speed to make it through the gate of the Downtown Manhattan Heliport. She'd judged it with such nicety that she'd barely scraped the driver's door, fitting the big vehicle through an opening only a few feet wider than the Suburban itself.

He got it now. She was slamming the monstrous limousine through the same maneuvers. There was a reason they called it "The Beast." With all of its armor and defense system, it was eighteen feet long, six feet high, and weighed in at eight tons— over twice his pickup with a full load. And she was making it spin and dance like it was a turbo-charged hotrod.

On the next run, she slammed it through a full three-hundred-and-sixty-degree spin, a full time around.

"Now why would she do that?" George mused aloud.

Jim glanced at Ralph and saw the small smile there, so he kept his mouth shut.

Reese did it three more times until she could nail the final direction every time.

On the next spin, when she was halfway through and facing

away from them, he saw a pair of canisters shoot out of the front and blast out a cloud of smoke as she continued her turn.

"Is that tear gas?" The wind was drifting their way.

"Normally," Arturo growled. "Just smoke canisters for training here."

"She laid them down as a blind to anyone following rather than to clear a crowd blocking the way," McKenna said almost reverently. It was clear he'd never thought to do it himself.

Jim felt an itch. That was Reese Carver at the wheel. And it was clear that she was angry at something. She was slamming The Beast around like it was part NASCAR racer and part demolition derby.

"Anyone willing to bet a twenty she has another trick up her sleeve?"

They all turned to look at him for a long moment, then looked away.

"Aw, c'mon guys. Easy money." Even making clucking chicken noises didn't get him a taker.

As if Reese could overhear their conversation, she started her next—and he'd bet final—run from the far edge of the pavement.

What if instead of going into a drift to turn ninety degrees as she had at the heliport gate, she first wanted to blind those following her?

She gunned toward them from the far end of the field. For a quarter mile, she let the lumbering Beast gather as much speed as it could.

Then just as the guys were starting to get nervous, wondering which way they'd need to dodge and run, Reese slammed into a spin.

When her car was turned exactly one-eighty—with its rear end facing them—she launched another pair of smoke canisters out the front. Because they were standing on her side of the smoke screen, they could see the car continue to spin until it was headed off to the left at speed—a three-quarters turn nailed perfectly on dry pavement.

If it was a T-intersection, the attackers might barrel straight through the smoke screen and crash into the end of the road. If it was a through-intersection, they might race straight through and across the intersection in hot pursuit.

Either way, the Beast wouldn't be there. Masked by the smoke screen of the tear gas canisters, she'd be gone in an unexpected direction. Sideways.

There was an awed silence among the observers as Reese continued down the narrow side road she'd entered. Then with one more hard thrum of the engine, she came racing toward them backwards before flipping the car through a final J-turn and coming to a stop close beside them.

Reese sat there holding the wheel and staring at him as he started applauding.

———

REESE WOULD RATHER Jim wasn't here. He wasn't supposed to be here. He was *supposed* to be at the White House, walking his precious fence line with his precious dog doing their precious sniffing. He—

She wanted to pound on something. Or someone. Jim was fast becoming a candidate as he led the applause.

How the hell had she gotten in this trap?

Miss Watson was right—it all somehow fit. *Reese* had been the target in New York. And for that to happen, it had to be an inside job. Which meant that she could trust no one! Once again she was out on the track all alone and no one to turn to.

She eased off the brake and, letting the idling of the big diesel engine put the car back into motion, drove along the small access road to the garage. She parked it by the other vehicles and turned off the engine.

A figure came up on the other side of the five-inch ballistic glass to open her door. She waited for Jim to fail. The Beast's doors didn't open by merely pulling on a handle—then any fool could run up and do it. One of the closely held secrets of The Beast was how to open its heavy doors from the outside.

But the door swung open anyway.

Ralph McKenna was standing there. He'd driven this car for a decade so of course he knew its tricks; he'd probably helped design them. The others were standing back a bit.

She popped her belt and clambered out, taking the hand that Ralph offered because she didn't trust her knees with how they were shaking. It wasn't fear. It wasn't stress. She didn't know what it was, but it was there and she didn't like it. She was such a mess that she should tell them here and now that she couldn't be the President's driver. Stagecoach—as the Beast was known whenever the President was aboard—was one rung of the ladder too high.

Ralph was no longer holding her hand, he was shaking it.

"When it comes time to put me in the ground, Carver, I want you driving the hearse. That way I *know* that I'll get to where I'm going."

"Not for a long time, McKenna." If the best driver in the Service told her that, it meant that she *couldn't* walk away. *Damn it!*

"Not a chance. I've got a cottage and a sailboat waiting for me in the San Juan Islands up in the other Washington. Time for me to go home. I know The Beast and his passengers are in the best of hands."

A double dare. Definitely no way out of it.

Arturo and George came up and shook her hand as well. "I can't see putting that in the standard training. I don't know if either of us could even do that move, never mind teach it to the poor *hombres* who come through here. Nice, Carver. Seriously nice."

Triple dare. Crap! All she'd done was drive. It was all she wanted to do. She didn't like whatever was messing with her knees.

Then they moved off and there was only Jim.

"Where's Malcolm?" She still wasn't ready to talk to him. She'd treated him like crap since New York and she wasn't ready to deal with that either.

"In the truck, sleeping off a hard morning of training," he hooked a thumb toward a big Dodge pickup with a crew cab and a short bed. Meant the thing was all for show because the bed wasn't big enough to haul anything. And it looked that way too, immaculately clean as if he spent the weekends polishing its glossy black surface.

On cue, Malcolm stuck his head up over the window sill and gave her a welcoming woof before disappearing out of sight once more.

"Can I buy you lunch? Know a good spot about ten minutes away. Great roast beef sandwiches. Beer if you're done for the day."

She was *so* done. Somehow he knew that she didn't want to talk about her driving. In the last five days she'd forgotten how easy it was to be around Jim Fischer. He never pushed her when she didn't want to talk.

"Fine." Her Pop would slap her butt a hard one for that kind of manners. "Thanks, that'd be great." A little better.

"Need a lift? Malcolm might insist that you sit in back..." he trailed off with a smile that appeared genuine.

She pointed at her ride, parked beneath a shade tree on the far side of the lot.

Jim glanced over his shoulder, then did a double take, which made her feel better.

"How did I miss that?" And he was on the move for a closer look.

At a loss for what else to do, she followed in his wake.

Pop had given her the rusting hulk for her fourteenth birthday, had it towed into the back corner of his racing team garage at the Motor Speedway. "You get it fixed up, honeychile, and you can drive it when you get to sixteen."

The 1969 Mustang Mach 1 had taught her not only how to fix a car, but why they worked the way they did. She'd torn the engine block of the Ramair Super Cobra Jet V8 down to bare metal and rebuilt it all the way up. The 4-barrel R-Code Holley carb had taken her a week to refurbish, and another three days before she figured out she'd put a float valve in upside down. Piece by painstaking piece, she'd put that car together with Pop's and his chief mechanic's training, but none of their help. It was all hers.

After a lot of soul searching, she'd decided to make everything as cherry original as she could until you lifted the hood. The engine, transmission, and suspension were all rebuilt with only one purpose in mind—speed. From the factory it would have run 0-to-60 in eight seconds. By the time she was done installing the nitro, it was well below five. Tuning the suspension had taken some work, but she could drag a quarter mile in the sub-ten-second range.

It had taken until she was eighteen to finish it, but by the time it was done, it was perfect. The jet black finish accented by a single, thin, red racing stripe down the side made it look fast standing still. The ram scoop in the middle of the hood, the rear louvers over the back window, and the rear spoiler made it look even more like a race car.

It was also the most fun ride she'd ever taken. A NASCAR

stock car was a faster, tougher machine, but it was pure race car. Her Black Beauty looked classic, but flew like pure joy.

"Damn, woman. Is this thing street legal?"

"Depends on the street." It was nice that Jim could see past the pretty car down to the fact that it was a performance machine.

"Bet that's faster than Road Runner being chased by Wile E. Coyote. What do you call her, Jackrabbit?"

"Black Beauty."

At that he went suddenly quiet and looked right at her, "Of course you do."

She was glad that her complexion would hide the heat rocketing to her cheeks.

"Okay," he didn't push it. "Can you go slow enough to follow me in my truck? Or should I give you the coordinates of the nearest airport for you to fly into?"

"I'll keep it in first and we'll see how we do."

Jim nodded and headed for his truck.

She liked that he kept it simple. Though she'd definitely have to razz him about going exactly the speed limit as he led the way.

CHAPTER EIGHT

*J*im knew it was a gamble, but he took Reese home.

"What's this?" Reese asked as she climbed out of the Mustang. No, as she oozed out.

All the stress she'd been showing at RTC until he was afraid to touch her for fear she might shatter had fallen away during the short drive in her Mustang. If he didn't get her out of that suit and into his bed in short order, he was the one who was going to shatter. But he knew a frontal attack wasn't going to win the day, so he'd just follow her lead.

"Home. Not much, but I like it." The way she'd eased down from her drive was exactly how this place always affected him. He'd sunk the money from selling his rig and being a good boy with six years of banking his Army pay to buy five acres just a half hour outside of DC and ten minutes from the Rowley Training Center.

Malcolm hopped down and ran around to see if any deer or rabbits had passed through since this morning's run.

It had been all trees. He'd hacked an acre-sized hole right out of the middle and parked his fifth wheel along the north edge so that he looked out on the sunny yard. A small stream ran at the far edge of the wide lawn.

"Got a nice wood deck on the southern side," he led Reese around to it. "Should be warm this time of day."

Reese kicked one of the tires on his fifth wheel as she walked by. "This thing ever move or are you like most RV owners who should just build a damn home?"

"Every vacation and the occasional weekend. Malcolm and I like wandering the backroads. Done a whole lot of Maryland and Virginia. Thinking to start Pennsylvania next. Hoping to do the original thirteen colonies, but really see them, not just the highways I drove back in my trucking days."

"That explains the big-ass truck," Reese muttered to herself.

"Have yourself a sit and I'll go rustle up some sandwiches," he waved toward the two loungers he had out on the back deck. He'd glassed in the sides to stop any wind. He had an awning he could run out, but rarely did—he preferred looking at the sky and the stars even when it got cold.

He headed inside and Reese came in on his heels. She prowled through the place, which didn't take long. There was the big bed up in the nose of the fifth wheel. The dividing wall that made it a bedroom had dressers below and a built-in big-screen TV above that could be spun on a swivel to face either the bedroom or the living room. One side of the living room had a two-burner cooktop, small fridge, and oven. The rig's only pop-out was the living room, which allowed for a big sofa and a couple of lounger chairs. Toward the back a bathroom and shower all-in-one, and a four-person dining booth that mostly served as his desk. There was a small outside swingout for a grill and a small storage bin that he kept stocked with wood for campfires.

"Not much, but all a man really needs." He began fishing out sandwich fixings.

Watching Reese prowl through the place was making it hard to concentrate. It had been a long time since a woman had been here. Maybe not since Margarite, and the contrast was startling.

Margarite had accepted that this RV and this property represented who he was—and that it wasn't her. She'd never really relaxed out here. Or around him, he supposed.

Reese filled the space with her presence as if she somehow belonged. She stood in the middle of the living room staring out at the lawn, backed by Loblolly pines and red oak trees, through the sliding glass door. She just seemed to soak it in. He knew that even if she never came back, it would take him a long time to get over looking at her standing there.

He concentrated on the sandwiches for all he was worth. He hoped that she liked the way he made them, because his mouth was too dry to even ask if she liked horseradish on her roast beef.

"Are you planning to look me in the eye anytime soon?"

He froze. He'd looked at her driving, at her hot car, at her in his rearview to make sure he didn't lose her on the way here.

"Seems kinda lousy of me not to, doesn't it?"

"It does."

"There's a problem though," he got his hands moving again. He finished the sandwiches, scrounged up a bag of chips that wasn't too decimated, and a pair of Cokes.

"What's that?"

"Look you in the eye, as likely as rain at a summer picnic, I'm gonna want to be kissing you."

That earned him silence.

Well, no guts, no glory. He turned slowly and looked at her. Those dark, mysterious eyes were watching him closely. Well, he'd been right. Even that brow-knitting expression she was wearing didn't change a thing. Three steps. That's all it would take, just three measly steps separated them.

"Even after the shit way I've been pushing you away all week?"

"Even after." He wasn't going to admit how much that pushing off had scared him—not even to himself was he going to be admitting that.

"Still feeling that way?"

"Seems I am." It was all he could do to not drop down on the carpet and drag her down with him.

"Dilya asked me if we were after the Meryton Hall dance or the Nettingfield Ball."

"Netherfield."

"She didn't explain herself."

"It means that either you've decided I'm a prideful jerk or that I'm actually dashingly handsome and alluring despite my vastly superior station in society."

"You walk a dog for a living," Reese rolled her eyes, but the frown had eased off to that cryptic partial smile of hers.

"You're nothing but a fancy chauffeur. Maybe we're in the wrong story."

"Not according to Dilya. So what's your role after the two dances?"

"Oh, I'm utterly fascinated by you either way, I'm just too shy to say so."

Reese finally laughed a little. "Shy isn't one of your problems. Being too nice might be one of them."

"Definitely the wrong story, then. So let's eat." Jim turned and picked up the sandwiches. He wasn't turning aside from the obvious path because he was too nice. Some instinct told him that going fast was going to make it "race over" way too soon.

Out of the corner of his eye, he saw her stumble a half step forward as he walked away. He hoped that was a good sign.

OUT ON THE BACK DECK, some part of Reese's sanity returned. She'd been within a moment of shoving Jim into that bedroom of his. It was right there, conveniently mere steps away. A man cave of dark woods and a big screen TV. Use his body, then leave him watching some ESPN.

She just wanted to lose herself in mind-blurring sex. Let a cathartic release help her forget, even for a moment, what Miss Watson had forced her to see.

Instead they were sitting on side-by-side loungers in the warm sunshine. The tall pines and oaks gave the property an other-worldly feel. It didn't seem possible that all the worries of DC lay so nearby.

Malcolm came back from his explorations, begged some roast beef from both of them, then curled up on a dog bed Jim had set close by his lounger.

The quiet of the place expanded, emphasized by the birdsong from the trees and even the quiet trickling of the distant brook, until it made her ears ring. Her apartment was in Friendship Heights and she'd forgotten what the country sounded like.

Jim knew that about her and simply ate. But it wasn't as if he wasn't there. Instead, her awareness of him grew and grew until it seemed as big or even bigger than the trap she'd fallen into.

"Get many visitors here?" Reese could hear cars, but they were so distant that she didn't hear them unless she was listening for them.

"Deer and rabbit. Got some moles over in the southeast corner that Malcolm catches on occasion. Had a coyote come through once. Raccoons come along to fish in the stream during the summer." His voice had a soft smoothness that made him easy to listen to but hard to keep track of the words. He was definitely talking about another world if those were his "visitors."

She considered as she took another bite of her sandwich. There *was* a very nice looking bed not ten feet away. But the sun-warmed deck and the canopy of blue sky were—

Jim reached across the gap between their loungers and took her hand. When she turned to meet his eyes, he was looking right at her. Not with a question, but with a need that she discovered she was sharing. At the slightest tug, she abandoned her seat and straddled over him.

Sensations jolted into her, even though they were both fully dressed.

"You doing something to me, Fischer?"

"Planning to, Carver."

It wasn't what she meant, but she leaned down to kiss him and decided to see how his plan went first—because all of hers were awful.

REESE CARVER in a darkened hotel room had been fantastic.

Reese Carver straddling him and silhouetted against the blue sky was a revelation. He opened her jacket and blouse, then blessed a front-opening bra. Every curve of her chocolate skin looked as perfect as it had felt. He filled his hands with her and still wanted more.

When she leaned forward and lay her bare chest against him, it was liking hitting that home run ball—just ever so sweet, knowing it was right and clean even before it soared aloft.

He tried to never make comparisons between women, but Margarite had never wanted to do it outdoors. She'd been a DC woman with DC aspirations. They hadn't even done it on the couch very often. With Reese it seemed as if everything was irrelevant other than their two bodies coming together.

When she disengaged long enough to shuck her pants, he saw that the wonder of her didn't end at her waist. She still wore jacket, blouse, and disengaged bra as she helped him shed his jeans and sheathed him before she moved back over him. Her sidearm in its shoulder harness rubbed the back of his knuckles as he once more marveled at the feel of her breasts and the contrast of his light hands on her dark skin.

Sliding into Reese was better than backing a double-trailer rig in a dead straight line. She moved against him with a rhythm all her own as her fingers dug into his shoulders. Her long hair slid from its ponytail and fell around them like a private curtain against the world. Only at the very last did her eyes slide shut, but he was unable to look away from the wonder of her. The line of her arching neck the moment before the release slammed into her and had her hunching to absorb the force of it when it arrived. The taste of her moan as he dragged their lips together before his own wild release had him arching up against her as if he could somehow bring them closer together.

Together.

Jim had never felt so *together* with a woman in his entire life. *This* was a woman that he could never tire of. It wasn't that she brought a new and unfamiliar spice to sex—although she did. It was that... Jim didn't know what. What he did know was that he was permanently ruined for any other woman.

When Reese finally eased down against him, he could only

marvel at the warmth and softness of this "hard" woman. Though the butt of her FN Five-seveN sidearm digging into his armpit argued the point the other way. He managed to slide it free and lower it to the deck.

She curled against him, burying her face in the crook of his neck.

He ran his hands up and down her back under her clothes. At first it felt as if she was merely snuggling. But he knew what a snuggling woman felt like and this wasn't it.

Somehow he was holding the "hard" woman again, even as she lay so completely against him. Reese was holding herself rigidly. As rigidly as he expected she'd been while putting The Beast through paces that no one else had ever seen before.

"Something you want to be talking about, Reese?"

She shook her head sharply enough to nearly bruise his jaw.

Maybe if he just held her a long while, she'd find what she needed—and he didn't mind that solution at all.

His bare legs were getting cold despite the warm sun. When he ran his hands down over her bare behind, it was covered in goosebumps. He tried chaffing her skin and it earned him a snort of laughter.

"If we don't move soon, you're gonna freeze the Secret Service's finest ass...et," he teased her.

It earned him a soft thump on the ribs, but then she unwound herself from him. She started reaching for her clothes, even holding her jacket closed, and he didn't like that at all. He scrambled to his feet, scooped up all of their clothes, and headed inside. Bare-assed, she followed, then doubled back for her sidearm.

He turned for the bedroom, dumped their clothes on the floor, shrugged off the few bits he was still wearing, and slid between the covers.

Reese stopped in the doorway and looked down at him—one hand holding her jacket closed and the other holding her sidearm. The hem of the jacket and blouse danced along her hips.

"You expecting something more, Okie?"

"Don't mind being comfortable while we're talking."

"Talking?" Reese eyed him skeptically.

"Talking. Oh, I got no more complaints than a tornado in a trailer park if you want to just have more sex, but I'm thinking that something's eating at you and this is as good a place as any to do the talkin'." He liked her smile when he really laid on the accent. Something about it worked on women and he wasn't the complaining type.

She hesitated for a long moment, then sighed. With a single shrug, she shed all the layers off her shoulders at once and stood like a black Madonna—an armed black Madonna.

Reese slid the sidearm under the other pillow and tucked into the bed beside him without a single point of contact.

"Now that ain't no way to be talkin'." He pulled her in until she lay against him with her head on his shoulder and her leg over his hips. He began toying with her hair. "By the way, you ever cut this and I'm throwin' you out with the dog."

"You don't lose that accent and I might do some cutting myself." She lifted her leg and slid her hand down around him to indicate precisely where she'd be trimming things.

"Whatever you say, ma'am."

She growled a little but left him intact, resting her palm once more against the center of his chest. Again she let the silence stretch a long time and he could feel her gathering her thoughts like the air gathering its strength. He just hoped that he survived the tornado when Reese unleashed it.

"Can I trust you? How can I trust you? And I'm not talking about sex."

"Didn't think you were," though he'd bet it would be easier if she was. "Always figured that had to be earned. Malcolm and I do our best to do that."

———

AND SOMEHOW THAT MADE A DIFFERENCE. Malcolm clearly trusted Jim for everything and Jim had won that trust through action and kindness.

"I'm in trouble."

She'd never understand how Jim's silence always helped her along. She'd always depended on men to pry out what they needed to know, because it was far safer to keep the rest to herself. But Jim simply waited for her own thoughts to form until she was ready to give them a voice.

"What if the attack in New York wasn't an accident?"

"Didn't think it was."

"What if it wasn't an attack either?"

"But—" then he stopped for a long moment. "A trial run?"

"That's what I thought at first. Then Miss Watson suggested—"

"Who?"

"Doesn't matter," Reese wondered just how few people knew about the spy in the White House basement. "What if it was a test?"

"A test," Jim rolled it over his tongue like he was tasting it. "A test of the Motorcade's defenses?"

This time she decided to keep her thoughts to herself and pray that Jim didn't reach the same scary conclusion she had.

"No. If it was a test, they were testing for something that they didn't know. You. They wanted to test what you could do, because you're what they don't know about."

She tried to stay perfectly still, to not give away her next thought. But she felt it along the entire length of their bodies lying together when the realization hit him.

"It's an inside job," he barely whispered it. "The truck wasn't stolen until after the New York team was mobilized. And to have it in that place, at that precise moment... But the Secret Service never had a traitor before..." The way he tapered off said that he agreed that they did now.

And that was the moment that Reese knew she could completely trust Jim Fischer. They were lying too close together for his shocked reaction to be faked. And his first, instinctive reaction was to crush her against him as if he could somehow protect her by simply holding her close. As if he could take the bullet to spare her.

The last man to protect her unconditionally had died in a shattered stock car.

Since then she'd forgotten what it felt like—had always relied on herself alone.

Then Jim sealed the bargain with a whispered question.

"What are we going to do?"

We. Not her. *We.* She could definitely get to like the sound of that.

CHAPTER NINE

*J*im had asked for time to think about Harvey Lieber's offer to join the mobile team of the Presidential Protection Detail. This morning he and Malcolm marched straight in and took the job.

He and Reese had brainstormed through the long afternoon, then over a dinner of delivery pizza—his five acres in the woods wasn't *that* far from DC civilization. Malcolm had gotten his usual pizza crusts from Jim—Reese ate hers. After dinner, they were still nowhere on figuring out who else to trust.

It was an odd problem. The Secret Service trained them to trust no one except the other members of the team. But when it became impossible to trust the team...

He'd favored telling Captain Baxter—the man had run the White House branch of the Uniformed Division for four Presidents and been Jim's boss for three years.

Reese didn't know him from Adam and favored telling Harvey Lieber. He'd been with the President for nine years, ever since Zachary Thomas had been nominated for the Vice

Presidency. But he'd always struck Jim as an unimaginative hard ass. He'd also been the one to personally promote Reese into her new position. Had that been a setup?

For the moment, they'd decided to keep everything to themselves.

They'd had sex again last night, but there was an overlay of tension now. Despite what the movies portrayed, being in fear for your life and suspicious of everybody did *not* enhance sex—not even in a them-against-the-world unity. They'd held each other close, but neither of them had slept well. Breakfast had been a fast and silent affair of leftover pizza. And the RV's shower wasn't built for two, even if they'd been in the mood.

"Welcome aboard," Harvey shook his hand and waved him into a chair. Malcolm plopped down at his feet as if the transition from Uniformed Division to the Presidential Detection Detail was the most normal thing in the world. He just hoped to god it was.

Baxter looked in, saw what was happening, and cursed. "Hate to lose you, Fischer. Make me proud." Then he was gone, back to his office with just that much ceremony.

"I'd like to give you a manual for your new duties, Fischer," Harvey was tapping his fingers together. "But we don't have one. We've never embedded a K-9 team inside the Motorcade before. They always travel ahead to prep the site. I've got reports of your work during the First Lady's trip, both prior to the event and during the event itself as well as your scores from yesterday's refresher training."

Jim didn't like that Harvey was still calling it "the event" rather than "the attack." Just because they couldn't confirm the latter didn't make it any less true.

"I'm assigning you to Agent Reese for now. You won't ride in Stagecoach, but she's already familiar with some of your methods. Tad Doogan is the head of the Motorcade, but he has enough headaches at the moment without adding another direct report agent to his list. I want you to work with the team and figure out how you fit into our processes."

"Yes, sir." Jim also didn't like that Harvey didn't refer to Malcolm, though he was sitting right there. Baxter would have said "you and your dog" or "you and Malcolm." Harvey acted as if Malcolm didn't even exist. With each passing second he was feeling better about advising Reese not to talk to him about their conclusions.

"Two more things. First, you do anything to screw up the efficiency of my Number One driver and you'll be walking patrol at a sewage plant." His tone made it clear that they were no longer discussing any on-duty actions.

Jim thought they'd been circumspect, but apparently not enough. Or did it somehow show on him? What would show? That he was completely gone on Reese Carver? He'd sure been wearing a goofy smile yesterday—Reese had commented on it a couple times. She didn't smile much, but she'd certainly come back to his bed for more, so it was hard to complain. But the tension today had wiped that smile off his face. At least he thought it had.

"Two, you've got forty-eight hours to get integrated into the team. "

When Jim looked at him in surprise, Harvey's grin was as plain evil as a rattler's.

"The President will be going to a new exhibit dedication at the flight museum at the Udvar-Hazy Center two days. From there, he's flying to Nashville to address the Cattle Industry Convention on his way to a triple header in his home state of Colorado. First, a speech at his alma mater of the Air Force Academy. Then on to the Olympic Training Center to have lunch with his mom, she's a swim coach there, and this year's athletes. Finally, a party fundraiser in Denver. Every stage has ground transport. Hope you like the hustle, boy." And Harvey turned back to whatever his next crisis was.

Jim scooted out quickly to let Harvey get back to it. Now he stood in the middle of the bustling Secret Service Ready Room wondering what the hell to do next.

He dialed Reese. Harvey had said he was assigned to her. It would be nice to hear—

"What?"

"That's how you answer the phone?"

"Yes. Now, what?"

Jim could feel her glower over the phone.

"Waiting here."

And he'd bet that wouldn't last long. "I'm assigned to you. So, um, where are you?"

"HQ Room 304," and she was gone.

He stared at the phone for a moment and wondered how to read her. Was she angry? They hadn't discussed him coming over to the Presidential Protection Detail. Maybe he should have. Or maybe she was just busy? No one focused on the lane they were in harder than a race car driver. So now he'd been demoted to a distraction?

"You got to wake up with her, dude." It might not have included wake-up sex, but she'd felt absolutely incredible in his arms. Not sure when he'd be back here in the West Wing, he gathered up all of his and Malcolm's most essential gear before heading out the door at a trot.

Dilya waved at him from where she walked the First Dog along the North Portico as he hustled out the gate into Lafayette Square and turned east for the six block walk back to the Secret Service Headquarters Building where he'd parked his truck to begin with. She looked as if she wanted to talk, but he wasn't ready for some question about the nature of his relationship with Reese if it was modeled on Regency England.

He wasn't ready to discuss it with himself!

Had he really thought that he was ruined for all other women by a couple-three nights with Reese?

He had. Moreover, it was true. Yet they hadn't spoken a word about what was happening between them; it had all been about work or in a silence that passed for understanding. If only he knew that it had indeed been understanding and not a path leading out the door and onto the open road.

Damn it! They *were* following the plot of Dilya's story. They were definitely in a relationship, as sure as the give-and-take of Elizabeth Bennet and Darcy, and they definitely weren't talking about it.

"Not a lot of Presidential Motorcades in your day, Mr. Darcy," he muttered as he crossed 14th Street against the light. A high-heeled blonde in a dark blue jacket and skirt so tight that it screamed look at me, eyed him strangely as he passed her by. That he didn't even give her a second look told him just how completely Reese had moved into his head and locked down his libido.

He slotted his ID at the security desk and headed up to Room 304. Inside was what he could only call ordered mayhem.

Cubicles were grouped in clusters down one side of the long room. Small signs indicated their functions: Route Security, Building Security, Police and Military Liaison, Air Transport, and more.

A dozen different agents were huddled around a central table. Built into its surface were eight large flat screens. Five displayed different maps: DC, Nashville, and three screens that must be Colorado. Each map had a red route and several blue routes.

He spotted an area that was labeled Motorcade Personnel and dropped his and Malcolm's gear there before joining Reese at the table. She was in the thick of it and looked as if she absolutely belonged. She didn't acknowledge his arrival with even a nod but, as she appeared to be at the center of three different conversations, he wouldn't take it personally.

"SIDEKICK—" the President's Secret Service codename "—will be at the Udvar-Hazy Center for two hours," Tad Doogan's slightly nasal and very Harvard-haughty tone sliced into Reese's headache.

Even her tiny nod to Jim and Malcolm had been ill-advised.

"We're directly under the Dulles flight path. We'll move him by Marine One helicopter from the South Lawn direct to Udvar-Hazy. He is keynoting a brief ceremony to open the exhibit featuring the Combat Search and Rescue Sikorsky MH-60 that he flew during his service in Yemen, Somalia, and other classified locations. His old unit is having an on-site reunion afterward. We will then transport him again by Marine One helicopter to Andrews where he will board Air Force One."

"Why not bring Air Force One to Dulles?" Jim's question cut off every side conversation.

"And who are you?" Doogan did his best down-his-nose look at Jim. He had humbled entire teams with that look.

"I'm the Motorcade's new K-9 dog handler."

"And what do you know of the logistics of moving the President?"

Reese winced on Jim's behalf, but there'd been no chance to warn him about what he was walking into. Actually, she hadn't even thought to do so, which was yet another unkindness.

Jim had held her last night when she'd most needed it. All the prior day she'd been groaning under the load of new knowledge: safety, protection, and her inability to meet those needs. If she'd been even half a second slower to respond, the three leading women of the land would be a bloody smear on the concrete barrier wall of the FDR Drive in New York. But she hadn't been. And somehow Jim holding her had helped her come to terms with that.

"I know that flying him thirty miles in the wrong direction, from Dulles back to Andrews, wouldn't be my first choice for security. When I drove convoys for the Army, that was always a fear—they knew exactly where we had to go because there was only one road from Karachi to Kabul. But I see on each of your maps here that you have multiple routes in case of last minute changes. Bad guys *know* that the President always departs from Andrews Air Force Base. So, for once, I wouldn't." Jim shrugged easily as if he was impervious to Tad Doogan's ability to use his glare to burn a hole right through your ego.

"Actually," General Arnson, the commander of the Marine One helicopters, spoke up, "I'm going to agree with the young man. If we time the landing, we could taxi Air Force One into position here at the holding area from Runway 1R. It's one mile from Udvar to that point along a secure road inside the airport perimeter. Run a small Motorcade along that road, then get him in the air."

Apparently Arnson was also immune to Doogan's lethal abilities. But if she drove that short leg of the Motorcade, then she couldn't be in position in Nashville in time to be the driver there.

Doogan's glare was now boring holes in the table. There was a dead silence until he snapped out without looking up.

"Fine. Carver will drive Stagecoach from Udvar-Hazy to Air Force One. A relief driver will then move the car over to the service area at the east end of Runway 30 to load up on a

C-17 and reposition it in Colorado. We will have a second Motorcade pre-positioned in Nashville. Essential Motorcade personnel will be provided with seats on Air Force One so that they don't fall behind. That includes Jamieson, Walker, Carver, and I suppose whoever you are," he waved a dismissive hand at Jim. "Now would everyone just start doing your jobs." He aimed a final eye-launched laser at Jim before stalking off. Everyone else dispersed rapidly into smaller groups or hurried to their desks.

"He's a real sweetheart," Jim whispered once they were the only two left at the central table.

"That was him in a good mood."

"How's *your* mood?"

"I missed Malcolm. Thanks for bringing him by," she kept her voice deadpan as she knelt down to pet the dog. And she did feel better. The impossible vice of pressure across her scalp had eased the moment the two of them had walked into the room.

Jim offered a sigh as heartfelt as his dog's for not getting his own slice of pizza last night.

Not wanting to give away how glad she'd been to hear Jim's voice on the phone, she'd kept her responses curt so that no one else could read anything into them. Her body had jolted at his arrival, evoking a hot flush of memories of how skilled a lover Jim Fischer was. He'd made any of her inadequacies seem irrelevant or even nonexistent, though she knew better. She could feel the heat brushing her cheeks, so she momentarily buried her face in Malcolm's fur. The heat Jim's mere presence was igniting throughout her body would have to wait for later.

How odd to be looking *forward* to a lover. She looked forward to a race or a challenging drive. Lovers were mostly for briefly soothing frayed nerves or finding a release for whatever was bound up inside her and couldn't find any other outlet.

"It's too bad humans don't have engine rattles and exhaust pipes." If they did, she'd know exactly what they were thinking. What she *herself* was thinking. Instead it was all muddled up inside her, and Jim Fischer seemed to be the one causing more muddle than usual.

Jim was smiling in a way that promised a scatological thought was on his tiny, trucker mind. Not the kind of exhaust pipe she'd meant.

REESE CRACKED HIM UP. She saw everything as some version of a car, as if humans were so easy to diagnose. He wondered if her occasional humor was intentional. Of all the agents in the room, he didn't recognize a one he could ask. It was as if the Motorcade was a world that had somehow passed him by unnoticed for so long.

Phones rang, keyboards were pounded on, and a large calendar covered a whole section of one wall. An agent—with a habit of squeaking his marker in ways that were making both him and Malcolm twitch—was marking upcoming travel. Six-country, eight-day East Asian tour next month. Three days at the First Family's farm in Tennessee. A meeting on the Hill.

Each, he realized, required an immense mobilization of manpower and equipment. Layered on in separate colors were travels for other key protectees: Vice President, First and Second Ladies, Speaker of the House, a visit by the British Prime Minister. The more layers he saw, the more there were to see. It was a rare day where some element of the Motorcade wasn't on the move.

Before he hit complete overwhelm, he turned back to Reese and their next mission.

"So," he looked at the maps on the table, because if he looked one more time down her blouse as she knelt over Malcolm and admired the bra that he'd helped put there just a few hours before, he wasn't going to be thinking of anything except how soon he could take it off again.

"So?" She rose to her feet and looked at the projected maps with him.

"Primary Motorcade route," he traced the jogging blue line across Nashville.

"And alternates," she traced the red lines. "Some are designed to cross the main route so that we can bail out onto them if there is a traffic problem or a detected threat. Some don't and are true alternates in their own right."

"And you memorize them all?"

Her steady gaze said that was a given.

Right! Reese Carver didn't like repetitions of the obvious.

Had she pre-mapped a variety of routes through their relationship? He'd rather not ask.

"Where do I fit in?"

"I don't have a clue," Reese looked as if she was answering both questions, even though Jim had meant to be asking about the Motorcade.

"Okay, then, I'll start." He looked at her steadily and saw her eyes go a little wide.

"Maybe that would be good," she said it softly. Softly as in a bedroom voice. She was such a driven person that it had never occurred to him to take the lead in where their relationship might go—he'd been along for the ride and enjoying himself. Which might explain where Margarite and the other women of his past had gone, following their own lead with no guidance from him.

Well, he didn't like the idea of Reese Carver drifting away due to his negligence. He *hated* the idea of her with another man.

"When a dog team preps a site, we're done before the Motorcade arrives. By the time Sidekick or any other protectee shows up, we're typically done and gone. One or two will hang on to keep the site secure, but most of us move on to prep the next locale. We aren't embedded directly in the Motorcade by any prior standard of practice." He'd always preferred the fence line, but that hadn't freed him completely from site prep for the President's trips.

"The Motorcade," Reese tapped a few controls and the DC map was replaced with images of vehicles lined up across the screen. She swept her hands across the surface and split it into sections so that she could stack and enlarge them, now a long double line spanning two screens. "It's typically made up of twenty-five to thirty vehicles, if you don't count the motorcycle police."

"Seen it go by enough times," Jim studied the pictures. "Never knew you were one of the drivers." As if he was apologizing for not having noticed her sooner.

"We don't go looking for trouble," even though Jim was definitely giving her some. "But we're ready when it comes." She'd give it back twice as hard as he dished trouble out if it came to that.

He shrugged as if her threat was of no consequence. He tapped the image of the first vehicle to zoom in on it. A standard black sedan.

"Tell me about it," but he didn't seem to be talking about the vehicle. If he thought she was going to talk about anything else in this room full of testosterone-laden men, he had another think coming.

"That's the Route Car. It runs several minutes ahead of the

Motorcade, typically with a small fleet of motorcycle cops who stop to block intersections as needed. They make sure the route is clear. Pilot car is another sedan usually. Their job is to make sure we follow the planned route. Don't want to get lost or turn into a cul-de-sac with a thirty-five vehicle caravan on your tail."

"Then a bunch of cop cars and more motorcycles."

"We call them Sweepers. Sweeping along at the front to make sure the road is clear."

"Then another sedan," he started to brush the picture off the side of the screen but she pulled it back.

"Don't dismiss it. This is a key car—called the Lead Car. It's directly in front of the main package: Stagecoach and the Spares. It's my buffer if anything goes wrong. Guide, early alert, and offensive driving. They're the best drivers outside of the limos. Remember the guy who stopped the delivery truck in New York by slamming on his brakes and taking the crash himself? That's the Lead Car."

Reese closed her eyes and hung on to the edge of the table as she continued. Wished they were in a place Jim could put his arm around her as the images came back.

"That driver died yesterday. Some blood vessel in his brain was too damaged. He was getting better, talking to his wife, and it just let go. Killed him almost instantly. The first the docs knew was from her screaming."

If it had come down to that moment and *she'd* been the driver of the Lead Car, would she have done that to protect the First Lady?

She supposed she would have or they wouldn't have chosen her to drive Stagecoach.

Unless she'd been chosen for some other reason. The first woman to drive Stagecoach. Or the first one they thought was weak enough to let an attack through? She glanced around the room. Was one of these guys, her fellow drivers, setting her up for the fall? What about Doogan? She could hear him being snooty over the phone to some poor Colorado police chief who probably deserved better. Or Harvey? Or…

It was the road to madness.

"That's my car," Jim stabbed a finger down on it and it zoomed in to fill the screen.

"*What?*" Her shout was loud enough to silence the room. Even Doogan paused in mid-phone-snoot to glance over at her.

"The Lead Car. That's my spot," he said it more quietly and the other guys turned back to what they'd been doing, though they did keep glancing over.

"*That—*" she swallowed hard and tried to temper her voice. All she could picture was Jim in the car as it was battered and broken on the FDR. "In reality, Lead Car is probably the most dangerous position in the entire Motorcade. It's the last line of defense."

"But," Jim tapped the image again and it zoomed in until all they could see was a tire. He pulled his hands away rather than touching the screen again. "I'm with the Motorcade. In fact, I'm guessing that it's unlikely that we'd ever be separated from the main Motorcade. But I'd still be first to arrive. That means Malcolm and I can deploy while Stagecoach is still coming to a stop. We'd be able to check the immediate area for as much as ten or twenty seconds before the President steps out."

"We don't release Stagecoach's door until we're positive the zone is safe," but she wasn't paying much attention to her own words as she considered the implications. She zoomed back until the entire Motorcade was in view. Reese had thought he'd travel in a support vehicle, maybe back by the inevitable press corps vans. But each of those were specialist vehicles: ambulance, hazmat, mobile communications center… Each was crammed with personnel. The Lead Car usually had just a driver and a spotter in the front passenger seat. There would always be room for Jim and Malcolm in the back seat.

"You sure?" She looked at him carefully.

Something about him had changed. He wasn't just some Okie trucker with an unexpected set of skills in bed. After what they'd both witnessed, it would take an immensely brave man to ride in the Lead Car. Doubly if they were right and the run at the First Lady's Motorcade had merely been a test. Suddenly her dog walker was the Army soldier who had driven through war zones for a living.

Jim nodded down toward Malcolm. "We're sure."

She knew how he felt about protecting his dog. If he was willing to risk both their lives, then he really was sure.

Then he looked at her, straight in the eye with no evasion, no blinking. Just that totally male smile of his that said they were now on a completely different topic.

"I'm sure."

CHAPTER TEN

*J*im followed Reese up the back stairs of Air Force One and tried not to feel like he was getting ready to leave the planet. He was certainly headed for a whole new world.

He'd been able to watch Air Force One just taxiing into position as their Motorcade had raced along the back road from the Air and Space Museum. Even for that short distance on a closed road, over a dozen vehicles had been involved: Route Car, Stagecoach, the five heavy-duty Suburbans carrying various aspects of the Secret Service, the cluster of press vans, and an inevitable ambulance. Overhead he'd been able to hear the pounding beat of Overwatch—a Marine Sikorsky Black armed to the teeth.

"I don't even hear it anymore. It's always there," Reese noticed where his attention had strayed. "Keep moving or you'll get run down."

Now the rush was for everyone joining the flight to race up the back stairs in the time it took the President and the senior staffers to ascend the front ones. The plane would leave when he was ready, not when everyone in the back was.

The members of the press clearly knew that as they crowded up the stairs behind him, most carrying small suitcases. For himself, he'd tucked a toothbrush and a change of underwear into Malcolm's pack and called it good.

He'd never walked under a 747 on the runway before and it was daunting how large it was. Planes never seemed that big when walking to them along an enclosed jetway. But this thing was massive. It blocked out the entire sunset sky. He could feel the weight of the responsibility of the Presidential load far more than from his first short ride in the Motorcade. All this, all these people, were to make sure that one man traveled safely.

At the head of the stairs, Reese headed out the left-side door into a seating area that looked like any other business class section he'd had to walk past on his way to the cheap seats. A glance behind revealed that the press exited the stairs via the right-side door.

"They get a boxed-in area on the other side of the fuselage from us. Fourteen seats, paid for by their agencies in the hopes of getting some tiny scoop from the President. They can't enter the rest of the plane without a personal escort by one of Harvey's boys."

"Harvey's girls don't count?"

She ignored him and led them to a pair of seats. The seats were generous enough for Malcolm to join them on the area between his feet and Reese's.

He was starting to recognize the faces who came into their side of the aircraft: four members of the PPD led by Harvey Lieber and two of the other drivers. The rest were unknown to him, but were easily identified as being attached to the plane rather than the Motorcade. They wore blue uniforms. Over their left breast, their name was stitched in white. Over their right was the Presidential Seal with "Air Force One" stitched above it.

"Is it me or is the air in here getting a little thin?"

"It's not you," Reese offered. "I've only been aboard a few times. Mostly I'm on the C-17 transport with the vehicles."

He wanted to take her hand, hold on to some concrete evidence that he wasn't so far in over his head. But he was... and he knew it. Two days assigned to work with Reese. He'd pictured at least meals and two nights together to explore a little of what was going on between them.

That idea had died in the first ten minutes.

"Joining the Motorcade is normally a three-month indoctrination. You have two days, so let's get to work."

Meals had been eaten while standing up or studying videos of simulated attack scenarios. Each had come with a twenty-page manual of what to watch for, position by position. The response scenarios had taken less than two minutes, but he'd had to watch some a dozen times to see how all of the pieces were moving at a deep level of coordination. Once he'd spent a day doing that, Reese ran him through a video he'd already seen dozens of times, the attack in New York.

A journalist had also taken a series of superb photos and videos that hadn't been available during his initial debriefing. The photographer had caught the feeling—and detail—of being right in the middle of every moment of the attack.

Step by step, Reese led him through the entire event second by second, displaying all of the different angles on the various screens of the central conference table. Much of the team had gathered around—it was the first-ever attack on the Motorcade in history that hadn't been repulsed while still several blocks away.

Each instant had a coordinated action.

"If a crisis occurs while you are traveling within our company," Tad Doogan had said in one of his tones, "I would highly recommend that you remain in your vehicle. Such an action will vastly increase the likelihood of survival for you and your animal."

Jim had wanted to brush off the warning, but Reese's deadpan expression stated that she'd heard worse advice.

As the frame-by-frame continued, Jim began to realize that perhaps she and Doogan weren't kidding. The agents who had poured out of the flipped SUV that had been caught in the truck's wreckage had moved quickly and aggressively to create a zone of protection despite how badly they'd just been rattled. And they'd done it in seconds.

On Day Two, they'd taken him out to James J. Rowley Training Center, but this time it was a full Motorcade, not just Reese. They moved into the winding streets of the simulated residential neighborhood.

They'd placed an agent in the back seat of the Lead Car with him. "Want to observe how you and your dog react."

Jim had served in the Army for six years and done dozens of training exercises here at RTC, so he hadn't expected anything surprising. He should have. The Motorcade was an attempt to reproduce the security offered by the White House and Air Force One, except in a mobile form. It was an incredible experience.

Malcolm's main complaint had been when the agent riding with them had asked him to roll up the window just because it was thirty-six degrees outside.

Jim's main complaint was that for two nights he hadn't slept with Reese Carver. Somehow, both nights he'd found himself driving home alone and he didn't like it one bit. He'd have been glad to plummet into sleep beside her and wake up together just getting dressed.

Instead, they hadn't so much as brushed fingers since that one morning in his fifth wheel. Reese was deep in the task, so deep that maybe she didn't even see that she was pushing him away.

He'd always been a family-oriented guy, he knew that much —he saw more of his parents and siblings, who were scattered all over the country, than most of his coworkers did who grew up in Baltimore or Charleston and had family nearby. Having Reese beside him when he woke up in New York and the one night at his place had him thinking about it for himself as well.

Reese had made it damn clear over the last two days that he'd been far too naive.

He glanced over at her as Air Force One roared down the runway, powering its way aloft with a surprising rate of climb. He almost felt as if he was an astronaut pushed back in his seat.

Reese sat with her hands folded in her lap and her eyes closed.

"What are you thinking about?"

"Feels like a stock car coming off the line," her voice was soft and whispery with nostalgia. "Pressed back in your seat. Two, three, four hundred miles of a challenging race just waiting for you to push the envelope. To find the edge and ride it through the heart of the pack. I miss it sometimes."

"Ever think of going back?"

She rocked her head side to side without opening her eyes. "Got a taste for doing something more important. Saving the First Ladies. That was something. We did that."

"You did." That had been clear from the videos. If she had been a single moment slower to respond, the entire rear of the Suburban would have been crushed. That had been clearly demonstrated by what the truck had done to the nose of the following Suburban instead.

"You'd have done the same," she opened her eyes and

looked at him. It seemed it was the first time they'd had a moment to really look at each other in two days.

"I'm just a trucker, not—"

"Hate to break this up. You two are with me." Harvey Lieber was standing in the aisle by Jim's elbow. The climb had eased, though they weren't up to cruising altitude yet.

Jim hadn't realized how closely they'd leaned their heads together as they talked quietly over the four big engines' roar.

"Three of us," Jim popped his seatbelt and nudged Malcolm awake with his foot.

"Right," Harvey said dryly before heading up the aisle.

A glance at Reese. She didn't know what was going on either.

They passed through the luxurious guest area with eight seats for guests plus two more tucked in corners occupied by agents watching the guests. Lieber didn't stop as they moved past the staff area, a big conference room with eight executive armchairs and a line of couches along the wall encircling a sprawling table of walnut, or even the senior staff lounge where four people were huddled together debating something.

"Uh."

Harvey continued leading them forward past the galley and a doctor's office presently configured as a small conference room.

They were fast running out of airplane.

A naval officer sat in the last chair in the long hallway they'd been following forward. At his feet sat the black leather briefcase of the nuclear football—the launch codes and communications gear that was never more than a hundred feet from the President in case he had to launch a strike.

Across from him sat a massive black man who Jim was fairly sure was the head of Secretary Matthews' protection. His hands were big enough that he could probably break Air Force One in two if he needed to.

Jim considered turning and sprinting for the back of the plane, but it wasn't nearly far enough away.

Harvey finally stepped through a double door bearing the Seal of the President painted in gold on the mahogany.

There was even less air here than there'd been at the rear of the plane.

REESE HAD BEEN within steps of the President any number of times, but she'd never actually met him. As a driver, her job was to stay behind the wheel of the car and be ready to move.

Now she was standing in his unoccupied office.

"He'll be with you in a minute. Sit. Don't touch *anything*." Then Harvey stepped out and closed the doors behind him.

She looked at Jim in desperation, but what right did she have to look there for comfort? For two days she'd tried to rediscover herself.

She depended on no one.

She needed *no one!*

Yet she'd spent almost every waking moment with Jim and enjoyed every second of it. She'd learned to anticipate his moods, partly by watching him, partly by watching Malcolm. Jim's sharp mind had been revealed behind his easy manner as they'd dissected video after video.

The only way to keep her head clear had been to get away—steer clear of him each night. Which had worked brilliantly. She'd lain alone in her bed both nights, thinking of him. Wishing him there beside her. Missing his silence in which to explore her thoughts.

Now she didn't dare speak. The President's flying office

was a disorienting space—it felt twisted inside the square space. The President's chair was in the forward corner and a curved desk defined the power of the position by its sheer size within the small area. For visitors there was a single armchair near the hull and a curved sofa lined the other two walls. Anyone seated there would be a head shorter than the President.

Jim dropped onto the sofa as if it didn't matter and Malcolm climbed up beside him to rest his head on Jim's thigh.

Resigned, Reese was most of the way into the lone armchair when the door opened.

The President stepped in.

Jim jumped to his feet.

She tried to, but was past the tipping point and had to bounce off the cushion with all the guilt of a little girl caught playing in her parents' room.

"Stand up, Malcolm," Jim whispered and gave his dog a hand sign.

Malcolm rose to all fours on the couch and wagged his tail.

It earned Jim a smile from the President, which Reese felt was a good move coming off the start line.

Zachary Thomas was a tall man, with an open and friendly face—his Air Force background was clear in his bearing. He was closely followed by a man ten years his senior, former President Peter Matthews, now the Secretary of State.

"Hello, hello. Please sit."

Reese abandoned the chair and moved over to sit on Malcolm's other side on the sofa that wrapped around the wall. It was a long sofa, so perhaps she shouldn't have sat so close, but she liked being able to run a hand into Malcolm's fur. It reminded her of the few quiet moments the three of them had caught together over the last few days: a moment by the candy machine, a long silence as they studied a video while sitting hip to hip. Jim made it easy to treasure those brief moments.

She waited for the President to break the silence, which he did after only a few uncomfortable moments.

"I wanted to thank you both for the roles you played in saving our wives' lives. If you hadn't already been assigned to replace McKenna before that, I'd have requested you, Ms. Carver."

"Thank you, sir. It was a pleasure to serve."

"Except maybe during the accident?"

Reese felt the jolt and glanced at Jim, who grimaced.

"Told you," Secretary Matthews said casually.

"*Not* an accident. What leads you to that conclusion that it was an attack?" The President kept his tone casual, not showing the least bit of surprise.

She and Jim had agreed that they didn't know who to trust. But if they didn't trust the President and former President, what was the point?

"Too many coincidences. However, we," she glanced at Jim, who confirmed with a nod. It took her another breath before she could continue, "We have concluded that it was *not* an attack."

That got her both men's full attention. She wished it hadn't.

"Please believe that this isn't an egotistical statement, but we think the whole purpose was to test my reactions as a driver."

The President narrowed his eyes at her. But he didn't speak. Both men restrained what must have been a hundred doubts and questions. Instead, they sat on the edges of their seats and listened. Neither man was what she expected.

Damn Jim for his thinning atmosphere comment. She couldn't seem to get her breath.

"We believe, sir," Jim thankfully stepped in, "that they used the attack on the First Lady's Motorcade as an action-response test in preparation for an attack upon your own Motorcade."

"Why am I only hearing this now?"

"The timing, sir. To place a truck at that moment in that place indicates an inside job. We don't know who to trust, Mr. President."

"Reminds me of Emily," Secretary of State Matthews leaned back in his chair and smiled. "That's a very high compliment, by the way, Ms. Carver. She did something similar to Frank Adams, the head of my protection detail. That was shortly before my first wife's death."

The two men exchanged significant looks.

It had been before her time. All Reese recalled was that the immensely popular Katherine Matthews had died in a tragic helicopter accident. Their looks said there was little love lost there and that the truth was probably a very different story.

"Harvey," the President shouted.

Harvey Lieber opened the door and stuck his head into the room. "Find Cornelia and both of you get in here."

While the door was closed, the President continued. "If we don't count my wife and this guy here," he waved a negligent hand at Secretary Matthews. "There are no two people I trust more. Actually, I probably trust them more than you, Peter." It was a clear tease between two men who had been elected together and were now friends.

Secretary Matthews shrugged as if it was no skin off his back.

Reese felt Jim grab her hand for a moment deep in Malcolm's fur and squeeze it hard.

Trust.

It was a hard concept for her and he knew that. She wished that she understood him better. Or knew him better. Yet she trusted him, like no one else more than Pop. Even in front of the leader of the free world, he did nothing to try and bump her out of the lane. He made it clear that she was the force to be reckoned with, not him or his male ego.

Why she'd pushed him away the last two nights was now a mystery that she couldn't—

Harvey and White House Chief of Staff Cornelia Day entered and closed the door behind them. She was a slender, tall woman who had a lethal reputation. She ran the White House and the President's schedule like a metronome. There had never been a more on-schedule administration in history. Everything about her said DC elite: an immaculate dark blue skirt and blazer, perfectly tasteful makeup on a flawless complexion, haircut simple but perfect for her narrow face, and a Cordovan leather case for her tablet computer. Her nickname was "The Shark" and rumor said that even real sharks would never stand a chance against her.

Ms. Day perched on the far end of the sofa.

Harvey stood with his back to the door and his hands crossed in front of him.

"Tell them," the President ordered.

So they did. Harvey's scowl went dark, but he didn't say a word until they finished laying out all of their reasoning.

"Carver, you ever leave me out of the loop again, I'm parking your ass in a kiddie car amusement park. Both of you!"

Reese swallowed hard.

"Second," he turned to the President. "Reasoning is sound. I don't like it, but it makes sense. Not a hint from the—" Harvey spun to face her so quickly that she jerked back against the sofa.

He rubbed his forehead.

"What?" Until that moment Cornelia Day had restrained her input to a nod that had her collar-length, dead-straight hair pitching forward and back in a slicing motion as sharp as shark's teeth (Reese guessed that Jim would appreciate the metaphor). But Harvey's consternation had finally moved her to speech—a short, sharp command.

"NASCAR to my Motorcade. Draw me a roadmap, Carver."

"I left racing abruptly."

"Your father's death," Harvey nodded.

Reese had kept her mouth shut and let the press and everyone else believe that. But the President deserved the truth. She was having trouble facing Harvey, so she turned to the Commander-in-Chief.

"Putting my father's team sponsor in the hospital with a lug wrench after he tried to rape me as part of 'consoling' me over my father's loss. No witnesses. He didn't press charges, but he blacklisted me with the other team owners and I was left without a ride."

"Why didn't you press charges?" Ms. Day leaned forward. Despite her cold-blooded reputation, she appeared genuinely concerned and upset.

"I tried. The police dismissed it. He was an important man in NASCAR racing and the Charlotte business community. I'm a black woman who looks like this."

Reese wasn't conceited about her looks, but knew from experience that men were drawn to her for a reason. Even Jim had started that way. But he'd moved on. No mistaking that he liked her body, but he also liked *her*, which she knew she was being slow in processing.

"The police wouldn't even investigate. Besides it was a he-said / she-said and there was no evidence other than the beating I gave him. His punch to my gut and his throwing me around the room by my hair when I refused to cooperate didn't even show. I wear my hair this long as a clear fu… As a clear statement to myself of who is in control of my life."

"I'll fucking kill the bastard." Jim apparently cared less about language in front of the President.

In the telling, she'd forgotten Jim was sitting there beside her. She'd seen him quiet and sometimes frustrated, but mostly he was Mr. Pleasant with that big welcoming smile of his. His face was now dark with fury and his light eyes were as black as death.

She wrapped her hand around his in thanks.

"Don't," she told him. "He's not worth it. Besides, I did tell his wife, who has made it her life's mission to destroy his career and reputation. I suspect not because of what he did, but because I'm black. She's very 'traditional' Southern in all the worst ways."

"I could get to like you, Ms. Carver," the President said lightly to break the mood.

She tried to pull her hand back, but Jim had clenched it tightly, for all to see. Harvey didn't show any surprise, Ms. Day didn't show anything at all, and the President traded a smile with Secretary Matthews that was all too easy to read. It said, "Isn't that sweet?"

Well, maybe it was at that. But now was not the time to think about it.

"From there to my Motorcade," Harvey demanded through gritted teeth. Fury was clear on his face as well. It made her think better of Harvey as she understood his anger probably had very little to do with her holding hands with another agent in front of the President and a great deal to do with her past.

"I found a flyer stuck under the windshield wiper on my Mustang. I went to see a race...from the cheap seats. Only place I've ever called home was Charlotte Motor Speedway and I'd never seen a race from the stands. Now that all of the backfield was closed to me, it was the only way I had to get on track—buy a seat. The flyer was there when I came out. I figured it beat the dead-end future I'd seen myself skidding toward for that entire race."

"The Protection Force," Harvey groaned as if he was in pain.

"What's that?" The President asked while the Secretary chuckled. "What?"

"My doing, I'm afraid." Then Secretary Matthews must have spotted Reese's look. "Oh, not me personally. There's a little outfit called the White House Protection Force. One of my gifts to you, Zack. They're the ones who saved us all last month with Linda and Thor. In my book, there is no possible higher recommendation of Ms. Carver's skills than being picked by them."

Reese had certainly never heard of them.

"Who?" The President and Ms. Day asked in unison.

"Completely anonymous," Harvey complained. "I'd feel better if they weren't *always* right."

Reese wondered what else this Protection Force knew. She became very self-conscious of Jim's hand still holding hers. Did they know about how he cared for her? That was ridiculous, even she hadn't known that. Not until he promised to kill her three-years-past would-be rapist.

JIM WAS WATCHING Secretary Matthews throughout the exchange. This Protection Force might be anonymous to everyone else, but it was clear that former President Peter Matthews knew exactly who was behind the operation. Clear as mud on a hog, his father would say. Having hauled hogs in his early days, Jim knew that was pretty damn clear.

White House Protection Force. Somehow they'd reached out and plucked Reese Carver out of NASCAR, but she'd won her own way to the driver's seat of Stagecoach. There'd been no doubting her driving skills in the First Lady's Motorcade. And no doubting the look on McKenna's and the trainers' faces that morning out at RTC as she spun The Beast through paces it had never seen before.

It simply confirmed to him that she was special in so many ways.

"I just drive," he teased her softly while the others were debating what to do about this new threat.

"I do," she was paying attention to the other conversation.

"You're a goddamn miracle, Reese Carver."

She turned to face him at that. Her brow furrowed as she looked at him.

He could see a succession of emotions slipping over her beautiful features. Denial, the weight of the past, puzzlement, and finally a small flicker of hope as she whispered, "Really?"

"Really."

She swallowed hard and offered the tiniest nod that said she'd still need a lot of convincing.

"We should cancel this trip, Mr. President," Harvey was arguing.

"I refuse to huddle in fear, Harvey. That's the Protection Detail in you: lock me inside Cheyenne Mountain and let me out in four or eight years after I've turned into a babbling idiot. I'm not an Air Force captain because I hide from danger."

"But—"

"You're not an Air Force captain," Cornelia Day spoke up. "You're the Commander-in-Chief." She sounded as if she was offended at him acknowledging the lower rank.

"Drive straight ahead, sir," Jim spoke, though he hadn't meant to.

Everyone turned to look at him. In for ten tons, in for twenty—that was Mom's saying.

"I drove Karachi-Kandahar-Kabul for three tours, sir. And the answer is to be ready. The answer isn't to not show up in the first place."

"Could get to like you too, Mr. Fischer." The President turned to Harvey. "We're keeping the trip schedule. It's up to you and these two to keep me alive. Don't let me down or I'll be very disappointed."

Harvey nodded, but didn't move from the door.

The look he aimed at Jim made him wish that he still worked for Captain Baxter and was walking the fence line.

"You seriously think it's someone on my team?"

Reese didn't appear to want to talk, which left it up to Jim.

"When did you announce that Reese would be the driver for the First Lady's trip?"

"I told the team within minutes of when you left for site prep, but only our own people."

"Not the press or a public announcement?"

Harvey shook his head. "Not until the night before departure. And the route was never published, of course."

Jim nodded. "I had guessed that. We arrived in New York Tuesday noon to scout the locations. We met the First Lady's party at the heliport on Wednesday morning. We were an easy target anywhere in Manhattan, but it would have been hard to guess our route. The truck was stolen on Wednesday morning at four a.m. before the First Lady's party had even left DC."

"Thirty-six hours later," Harvey finished for him, "at 1600 hours on Thursday, the attack occurred. It was the one place they could be sure of our arrival route and time based on our public departure from the UN building."

Jim nodded. "Who knew about the trip in time for that truck to be stolen? Who knew our exact departure time from the UN and was poised to have that truck in the right place at the right time?"

"There's never been a traitor in the Secret Service. I'm going to find his ass and I'm going to grind him so far into the ground so hard that they'd need an oil drill to find his body." Harvey's snarl was one of the most dangerous sounds Jim had ever heard. No one faking it could make that sound.

Cornelia rose to her feet. "Thank you, Mr. President." Showing no fear, Cornelia eased Harvey Lieber aside as if he was an errant puppy and opened the door. She waved for them to leave, and Jim would have run except it took him a moment to understand that he couldn't disentangle himself from Reese's grip.

It had changed as they sat there. At first it had been comfort, no surprise to him at all that she'd successfully defended herself against some bastard rapist—he was just sick that's how she'd lost something she'd so loved. But now they were holding hands as if it was the most natural thing in the world.

And it was.

Jim had never been much of a hand holder. Margarite hadn't been either, which maybe should have told him something. So what did it say that he wanted to hold Reese's? Not to keep her close and safe—okay, not only that. But because he liked the connection there. Liked the way their fingers laced together as if they were the same hands despite the different colors of their skin.

As they rose to their feet, it was so hard to let go of her. And the President's knowing smile wasn't helping at all. He'd seen the President and his wife on TV—it seemed they were always holding hands. Holding on as if it was the most natural thing in the world.

When Reese finally noticed and went to extract her hand, he held on, earning him a puzzled look from her and a "good man" nod from the President. So he kept her hand in his as he led her out of the President's office.

Cornelia Day led them into the medical suite directly aft of the President's office. She shooed out the doctor and nurse. There were two chairs and a tiny couch. The operating table was folded up against the wall.

Ms. Day and Harvey took the two chairs; he and Reese were pressed hip-to-hip on the little couch, which he wasn't complaining about. Malcolm got the floor.

"Now. We're going to go through the entire trip step-by-step until it is second nature to all of us."

That's what they did for the entire hour-and-a-quarter-long flight to Nashville. And when nothing untoward occurred, Harvey and the two of them spent the next two hours to Colorado Springs doing the same thing.

They arrived at Peterson Air Force Base, Colorado Springs, at 2300 local time.

The President would sleep in his suite in the nose of Air Force One. Most of the Protection Detail would stay aboard as well, but the Motorcade personnel had no reason to remain aboard through the night.

Colorado Springs was at six thousand feet, almost a thousand feet higher than Denver, and was bitterly cold. A several-inch dusting of snow lay on the semi-arid desert.

All the vehicles of a second Motorcade were already pre-positioned inside the hangar, ready for tomorrow's events. Not being on duty until shortly before the Motorcade would have to roll, they grabbed a base car and headed for the nearest hotel.

CHAPTER ELEVEN

*R*eese had never been like this with any man.

They played grab-ass at the registration desk.

They would have had sex in the elevator if it had been more than two floors or in the hall if they'd been at the far end.

As it was, while he battled with the keycard, she stood behind him. Peeling back the coat she'd opened in the elevator, she yanked out his shirt hem and ran her hands over his flat stomach and up his chest, pulling herself hard against his back.

He had a workout chest, the legs of a man who walked for a living, and hips that her legs fit around like they'd been made-to-order.

Why in the world had she been avoiding that?

The *sha-shink* of the releasing lock was the only cue she needed to shove him against the door, pushing it open with his body. It was a good thing that Malcolm was fast on his feet or he might have been locked out in the hall and she'd have been helpless to pause long enough to let him in.

Jim let her pin him back against the wall. There was no

questioning that he let her because even as strong as she was, he was in a whole other category.

"Reese?" Jim's voice was tentative. Cautionary.

"Don't you get," she spoke between attacking different portions of his and her clothing. "There are times when you don't talk. All you do. Is get naked." Both of their sidearms hit the floor with a heavy thump.

"This is one of those times?"

She finally had his pants off and grabbed him. The way he filled her hand was amazing.

He grunted hard into their kiss when she simultaneously rammed their mouths together to stop any more words.

Okay, perhaps she'd grabbed him a little too hard, but he felt so incredibly good. So powerful. So...male. For the first time in her life she actually wanted all she could get of his pure, unadulterated maleness.

It wasn't his anger at how she'd been treated in her past that wowed her—she'd already known he wasn't one of those guys.

It wasn't the way he stood up for her at every opportunity —though that was sexy as hell on several levels.

It was... She didn't know.

That almost stopped her.

She wasn't a wanton, not by any stretch of the imagination. But Jim Fischer made her feel so free at the moment that she wished she was one. Just for him. Even if it was just this once.

"I'm not stopping," she told them both, then gave him another squeeze to prove her point. "You going to do something about it, dog boy?"

"Well, if you insist." He kicked his shoes and pants free. With a shake of his arm, he managed to shuck the last of his shirt and jacket off his wrist. Then he squatted down just enough to shoot an arm between her legs. One hand grabbed her butt, the other wrapped around her shoulders; he scooped her aloft as if she weighed nothing.

Three steps later, he *threw* her down on the bed. Hard enough that if it had been a better mattress, she would have bounced.

"Ready?"

"Stop talking!" She was breathless from the magnificence of him. From that moment of flying before she'd struck the covers—floating loose in the instant before a gear shift once more threw power into her system.

And he did stop talking. He fell on her. His hands...his mouth...were everywhere.

Faster than had ever been possible, he drove her aloft until everything came apart.

But he didn't stop there.

Again and again he showed her just what was possible, then found a new way to break through the envelope and find even more performance from her fracturing nervous system.

He stuck to her like perfect racing slicks on a hot track until she couldn't know what was coming next and could only hang on for the ride. When he finally took her, when he finally pounded into her, there was little more left in her than a whimper.

But it was a whimper of joy from the body, not from her. Deep inside her, down at the heart of her body's engine, it was so much more.

Somewhere inside her, the past was burning away.

That bastard who had thought rape was his due.

Gone.

The drivers who had harassed her on the track...crowded her car into corners so that she ate a wall and was out of the race...who had done everything they could to prove that a woman didn't belong in a man's sport.

Blown away.

All of the times she'd somehow thought it was her fault. Her fault that she'd cracked up another car, even though they were always tapping her rear fender to break her loose. Her fault that she had come in second, not first, despite the on-track battles she'd surmounted. Her fault that...everything!

Gone!

Jim Fischer had just shown her that, in his book, there was no woman who deserved more. That she was special beyond her body—that it was only the stock equipment that he'd driven like a master tactician to prove to her who she might one day become, beyond her body's performance specs. There was a glimmer of light there that she'd never seen before.

Never imagined.

Yet Jim's passionate need for her had revealed it as surely as lights illuminating a nighttime racetrack.

She clung to him. A tangle of limbs in a cheap hotel, unable to let go, unable to ease up her double-armed throttle hold around his neck. All she could presently do was feel and know that she held one man—one fantastically special man.

CHAPTER TWELVE

*J*im glared at the tires in frustration. The night had brought a fresh dusting of snow that was slick to walk on. Which meant it would be slick to drive on. Not what he wanted on his first real mission with the Motorcade.

Colorado Springs road crews had already sanded the primary Motorcade routes and were reportedly working on the alternates…drawing massive "shoot me here" targets to his way of thinking.

"At least they've put on studded snow tires," he tried to find the bright side of it all, but wasn't having much luck. Apparently chains would be a major problem if someone shot out the tires and they had to get away on the run-flat tires. Each one had an inner core of hard rubber, but if the outer tire deflated, then chains would become loose and could create a snarl. That had meant a change of tires. At the moment he wasn't feeling very happy about *anything* changing.

"It will alter my spin rate, if I need to do one," Reese seemed to be taking everything about the morning in that easy stride of hers.

He could only glare at the car as Reese headed off to consult with the other drivers. No question that his mood was foul this morning. And no question that he was doing a crappy job of hiding it from Reese. Even Malcolm had picked up on it, moping about his feet.

"I should have stayed on the goddamn fence line." He understood *that*. He knew what to expect there.

Everything was confusing now. He'd spent two days trying to inhale Motorcade logistics but it was such a massive task that an entire vehicle was dedicated to just that. The ID car might run well back in the pack. Its sole task was route logistics and identifying any problems and changes on the fly.

So, he needed to let that go.

Even identifying his own role here was a challenge. He wasn't on the drop-in ahead team, patrolling a route, building, or crowd. He deployed twenty to thirty seconds ahead of the President as if that was enough time to find anything that all of the other dogs had missed. It made no sense.

Yet Harvey Lieber had asked him to join the Motorcade itself. Because a single time he'd been faster thinking on the ground in New York than most others? That had nothing to do with Malcolm. It had nothing to do with the last three years of his life as a White House dog handler.

"What's gonna become of us, buddy?" Malcolm looked up at him, clearly bored out of his skull. They were usually never bored. Not when they had the whole fence line to patrol. No tourists here inside the Peterson AFB hangar. No veterans in need of a little cheering up. No bad guys thinking they could directly breach the White House and live to tell the tale.

"C'mon, let's check out the cars. *Such!*"

And at the simple seek command, the life surged back into

Malcolm. He jumped to his feet, glanced up at Jim until he pointed toward the front of the parked Motorcade, and headed off with the same joy he walked the fence. The vehicles were lined up in three parallel rows so that they all fit in the hangar.

"You've got it way too easy." Malcolm only had one thing in life to worry about. For himself, he couldn't seem to stop finding new things to add to the worry list. It was already longer than an elephant's leash and it just kept growing.

They circled both of the Spares and Stagecoach itself. Then they went over the Lead Car that they'd be riding in. The police escort was already in place, so he checked out their motorcycles and Sweep Cars. He even went over the Pilot and Route Cars, though they'd be well ahead of the Motorcade to provide early warning of any problems.

Reese joined him as he circled back down the far side of the line.

And the anger surged back in so hard that he almost choked.

"What?"

He could only shake his head. He didn't know! It wasn't at Reese, he knew that much, but he couldn't seem to put a good face on it—not even for her sake. It wasn't her past. The assholes in her past were obviously losers who'd never understood what she was. She'd survived them and come out shining.

There was no real way for Malcolm to inspect Halfback. It was in line directly behind Stagecoach and the Spares and was armed to the teeth. It was filled with weapons that were fired frequently and with the men who fired them. They even had explosives, just in case they needed to cut the President out of a wreck quickly. Still, he gave Malcolm a treat each time he triggered on the vehicle. It wasn't his fault that they lived in a crazy world that needed such things.

"Did I do something wrong last night?" Reese kept her voice low as they moved on to inspect Watchtower—the electronic countermeasures Suburban. It could block signals to IEDs, detect incoming aircraft or missiles, and a wide variety of other attacks. If anyone fired on the Motorcade, they'd discover to their dismay just how fast Watchtower could pinpoint their location and transmit it to Hawkeye Renegade— the counter-assault team vehicle farther back in the lineup.

"How could you possibly think that you did anything wrong last night, Reese?" He couldn't quite bring himself to look at her. That was okay. He had to pay attention to what Malcolm was doing, didn't he?

"Because you're being very weird this morning."

"Well it's not you. Okay? I couldn't imagine you being more incredible. You're a goddamn fantasy brought to life."

"I don't want to be someone's fantasy. I've had enough of that shit!" The anger shot to life in her voice.

"Doesn't keep you from being one." Reese Carver was certainly his fantasy. Gorgeous, amazing in the bedroom, skilled, intelligent, thoughtful... The best companion a man and his dog could ever ask for.

"Eat hot shit, Fischer!" And Reese spun on her heel and walked away.

"Well, that went well, didn't it?" he asked Malcolm. Two of the agents managing the senior staffer vehicles looked at him in surprise, then turned to watch Reese. Even pissed as hell, she had an amazing walk from behind. Only by gritting his teeth did he manage to avoid beating the crap out of them for staring at her so blatantly.

Thankfully Malcolm was busy working and didn't know enough to roll his eyes at Jim.

"Yeah. Total washout." He guided Malcolm down the line: Control, counter assault (which gave Malcolm just as much trouble as Halfback had), intel division, hazmat, Roadrunner (that could connect them to a satellite feed, into the Situation Room, or provide a local cell tower when there wasn't one), ambulance, and the rear guard vehicles.

About the time he reached the end of the last line, the two press vans rolled in, bringing the press corps back from their hotel. They tucked into the back of the middle row of vehicles so that they'd be in the right place for departure. The reporters moved clear, winding their way past the inner row of vehicles. They gathered around the base of the steps of Air Force One (there was a scheduled ten-minute press conference before they moved out, not as if anything had happened overnight). He and Malcolm moved in to check the vans.

Clean. Clean. Clean.

If he found one more thing that was clean and safe and secure he was gonna scream.

That was the problem.

They *knew* there was an attack coming. It was coming and there wasn't anything he and Malcolm could do about it. How was he supposed to protect the President? How was he supposed to protect Reese, when any threat was so far out of his league? How was he supposed to find explosives from *inside* the Lead Car?

He squatted down to give Malcolm a good rub. At least his dog would know that whatever happened, it wasn't his fault.

He squatted there, in front of the lead press van. There were two of the Chevy Express twelve-seaters. They were big enough, barely, to carry the press corps and their gear. It was the last of the all-American boxy vans. Even Ford had taken on the slick Euro-Japanese exterior profiling. He'd driven the delivery version of the Express plenty before he'd gotten old enough to pick up his commercial license and move into the big rigs.

There was a small box under the steel bumper that he didn't recognize. He leaned in to inspect it. A Brickhouse Security micro camera, smaller than a pack of cards. It could shoot eight hours of HD video without a recharge. As far as he knew, they only saved to an SD card, but could one be modified to transmit? That hadn't been included in his briefings about the Motorcade, but he'd come aboard so recently that it could be just one of a thousand things that there hadn't been time to learn.

He leaned out and saw that there was a matching one under the second van's bumper. On the next row of vehicles over he could see that neither the intel car nor the hazmat truck had them.

Turning the other way, he could see one under the bumper of Stagecoach. He was pretty sure that wasn't supposed to be there.

He pointed out the small camera to Malcolm, *"Verloren."* Lost. Maybe whoever had put them there had left the same scent on each of the cameras, just as Jurgen had left his scent on the explosives out at RTC. If they were all the same, that would be very suspicious. After Malcolm had a good sniff of it, Jim gave him the seek command and they began circling the vehicles once more.

REESE TRIED to think of the last time she'd felt this angry. All she could come up with was her pop's former team owner. Jim had made her feel so...violated!

Last night had been such an incredible experience. And this morning she was just another hot fantasy calendar girl only fit to be a pin-up on some testosterone-laden grimy garage wall—her butt and breasts eventually coated in oily fingerprints from every mechanic who slapped it as they walked by.

One thing was certain, Jim Fischer was never going to touch her again.

Rather than feeling righteous, she felt impossibly sad.

"What the hell happened to you?" Harvey Lieber was suddenly at her elbow as she stood under Air Force One's wing with nowhere to go. She should be waiting by her car, but Jim was there, circling around them once more. Her interest in joining the press conference at the base of the plane's stairs was less than zero.

"I'm fine."

Harvey looked over her shoulder toward the Motorcade. "God damn it. I warned him."

"Warned him what?"

"That if he messed up my best driver, I was going to kill him."

"Don't!"

That earned her a Harvey Lieber scowl.

"I want the option to do that myself."

At that he smiled.

"Now I know you're okay. Get in your vehicle. We're almost ready to roll." Harvey walked over to join the President as he took last questions.

Okay? She was anything but okay. Though from Harvey's perspective, maybe she was. If she was head of the Presidential Protection Detail, she'd *want* her drivers to be in a foul, run-over-anything-in-my-way mood. And she was definitely that.

She stalked over to Stagecoach as Jim rose from looking under the front bumper.

He froze and looked at her. She could see there was some question written across his features.

To hell with him.

She opened the driver's door, slipped inside, and hauled it shut.

He came around to her window, the only one in the car that rolled down (though just three inches), so that she could talk to an agent or pay a toll if necessary.

Reese had no interest in talking to him and liked having the eight inches of armored steel and five inches of armored glass between them. Instead she placed both hands on the wheel and stared straight ahead. *Please, oh please. Let Jim Fischer get in her way.* She would run him down in a heartbeat!

SUDDENLY EVERYONE WAS on the move.

Jim had never seen the full Motorcade load up all at once and it was a daunting sight. Thirty-five vehicles including the police escort. Except for the motorcycles, most vehicles had four or five people. The press vans and the assault team Suburbans had even more. Two hundred people on the move in a highly coordinated flow.

One side of the hangar doors slid open and the Route and the Pilot Car shot out into the morning brightness. Now that the door was open, even though they were still inside the hangar, a phalanx of four agents surrounded the President as they escorted him into Stagecoach.

Once Harvey Lieber had the Beast's door closed, he came sprinting around the nose of the vehicle. He shoved Jim hard enough to send him stumbling forward.

"You aren't in your seat in the next five seconds, we're leaving you behind."

Even as he turned, Jim saw the momentary flash of the Lead Car's backup lights as the driver shifted from Park to Drive. He sprinted over and opened the back door.

Malcolm leapt aboard and the car was moving while Jim still had one foot on the ground. He dove in, landing partly on top of Malcolm who thankfully had gone to the far side of the back seat. By the time he had the door closed and his seatbelt buckled, they were already well away from the hangar and racing for the airport's nearest exit gate.

Mack and Mark—the two agents in the front seat—were laughing at him.

But Jim wasn't in a laughing mood.

For twenty-seven minutes all he could do was stare out the window and worry as they roared across Colorado Springs, up I-25, and finally, at long last, onto the supposedly safe grounds of the Air Force Academy.

He'd sworn he wouldn't look back at the three Beasts following on the Lead Car's tail. They were busy doing their dance, playing a game of Three-card Monte at sixty miles an hour to hide which vehicle carried the President.

But Jim always knew when Stagecoach was in the lead of the two Spares—he could feel Reese glaring at the back of his head.

REESE KNEW that she should have stayed in her car, but the President was giving a thirty-minute speech to the student body of the Air Force Academy north of Colorado Springs and then having an hour-long meet-and-greet with top class members and the school's commanders. Dry. Scattered trees. Snow dusted thinly among the brown grass. Freaking freezing beneath a brilliant blue sky.

The instant she was out of the car, Jim Fischer came over from his patrol. He'd been fast and efficient, in exactly the priority order that they had worked out over two days of planning. It was impressive how much ground he and Malcolm were able to cover between the moment of their arrival and when Harvey approved the site as clean and opened the President's door.

Somehow sensing her desire to duck back into the driver's seat, he signaled Malcolm to slip into the narrow space between her and the door, then waved him to sit and stay.

Traitor! I thought you liked me.

Malcolm lolled out his tongue in a doggie grin.

Trapped in the open, Reese forced herself to face Jim.

"I've got a problem."

"More than one," she shot back.

Jim chewed on that for several moments before discarding whatever he was thinking. "I've got a problem because I don't know what is and isn't protocol on the Motorcade."

Reese bit back her unexpected disappointment. He wanted to be strictly business and she wanted… She wasn't sure, but running him over with Stagecoach was still an attractive option. She waited him out.

"Are spycams standard on the vehicles?"

"What are you talking about?"

He took her by the forearm and it was all she could do to not yank it away in front of the other drivers and agents who had remained with the vehicles.

Fischer—that's all she'd think of him as now, except maybe Asshole—tugged her forward until he was standing well to the side of her car. The Motorcade was lined up in the parking lot alongside Fieldhouse Drive that they'd blocked off in front of the six-thousand-seat Clune Arena. Then he squatted and pointed under Stagecoach's bumper.

She squinted, but didn't see anything. Then she pulled off her sunglasses.

There, in the shadows under her car, was a small black box.

"It's a miniature HD spycam. I know the model. Fully self-contained: camera, battery, and storage card. It's set to activate in motion-detection mode. I brought you over here to the side because it and the others are all aimed straight ahead."

"Others?" Reese could feel her skin go even colder than she could account for in the chilly morning air.

"Press vans, all three Beasts, back of the Lead Car, front of the Halfback and Watchtower, front and back of the ambulance."

"Of the ambulance?" She turned to look. That didn't make much sense, nor did the press vans. There were a lot of vehicles between the Protection Detail riding in Watchtower and the press vans. "How did you find them?"

"Pure chance on the first one. After that, I had Malcolm sniff them out. Same person touched every one. And they weren't wearing gloves, so they left behind a clear scent mark."

Reese actually looked Jim in the eyes for the first time since this morning. And all she saw was the professional. Fine with her, that's all she should be seeing at the moment. Besides, the professional was someone she completely respected. She looked back at the camera attached to her car.

"I can tell you one thing. They aren't ours."

THE ELECTRONIC COUNTERMEASURES from Watchtower said they couldn't pick up any signal from the spycams, concurring with Jim's own assessment that they were set to record only, not to transmit.

That calmed everyone's nerves down.

A thorough visual inspection of all vehicles showed that Malcolm had uncovered every one of them, which had earned him high praise from everyone except Harvey Lieber—who was still too pissed at someone having messed with his Motorcade—and Reese—who was still pissed at Jim himself, but he couldn't take the time now to figure out why.

They'd been on the verge of pulling them, but Jim intervened.

"Look. Whoever placed these is getting set to record some event. Maybe it's just more intel on Motorcade operations. Maybe not. I say that we leave them in place so that whoever it is doesn't get suspicious."

Reese was nodding, "I'd rather face an attack today than if we spook them and they do it at some unknown time in the future." She glared at Jim as if he was the one doing the attacking.

"We just make damn sure to take down anyone who tries to recover them," Harvey snarled with all the danger signals of an ERT—emergency response team—attack dog.

Jim hauled Harvey and Reese aside.

"We still don't know who to trust. Now the entire Motorcade knows about the cameras."

"Shit!" Harvey wasn't happy.

"Not all of them," Reese put in. "Only the drivers and assault teams. The press, senior staff, and the protection details still don't know we found them. They're all in with the President. Nothing's gone out over the radio except my request for you to leave the detail and come join us."

"Well, that's something."

Jim scanned the area, but the Academy had made a point of emptying out the broad parking lot prior to the Motorcade's arrival. Beyond its broad expanse, the Front Range of the Colorado Rockies kicked up the land into rough slopes with sparse trees. A glance at the gymnasium and Jim could see a line of Delta snipers along the roofline—each studying a different section of the surrounding hills through their scopes. Nothing moving out there except maybe some deer.

He, Reese, and Harvey went down the line, verbally spreading the order that the cameras' existence was strictly need-to-know, compartmentalized information. Also that they were to keep their eyes out for anyone who went near one.

They met up once more alongside Stagecoach.

"Record only. Video only. What use is that?" Harvey sounded even grumpier.

Jim let his gaze drift down the long line of vehicles. They were in a double line outside the south entrance to the Cadet Field House. The first half of the Motorcade was closer to the building, with Stagecoach exactly aligned with the entrance doorway. The second half of the Motorcade formed a layer of shield from the wide empty parking lot.

An attack here on the Air Force Academy grounds would be very unlikely. That meant that if it was going to happen, it was still in this mission's future. There were four more pending sorties: Academy to Olympic Training HQ, Olympic Training to Air Force One, then, after a short flight to Buckley Air Force Base at Denver, out and return to the political fundraiser.

It would be an external attack again, otherwise there'd been no point in testing Reese's driving in New York.

"Someone wants images of the attack."

Reese and Harvey looked at him, but he didn't want to be distracted.

The spycams had been placed so that they would be focused on Stagecoach and the Spares. Rear end of the Lead Car. Front of all three Beasts. Front of the two vehicles immediately behind the Beasts. Then a long gap all the way back to the press vans and then another skip to the ambulance.

"They want to record the attack *and* the aftermath." Which

explained the ambulance. But it didn't explain the press corps' two Chevy vans.

He looked back at Reese.

"Those images of the New York attack. The ones that you had that I hadn't seen before, where did they come from?"

"Some news agency. I'd have to call Doogan to find out."

"Need to know?" Harvey cut in before Jim could.

Reese was already shaking her head because she figured it out just as fast as they had.

"But who put them there?" Harvey was starting to get back to focusing on the problem.

Jim shrugged. "A traitor inside the Service working with the Press would have plenty of access or..." He thought about the layout of the Motorcade in the hangar this morning and the Press Vans pulling up to the rear of the middle row. "That's it!"

"What's it?"

"This morning, when the Press Vans pulled into the Motorcade. The reports flowed out of the vans and wandered through the Motorcade to get to the steps of Air Force One for the President's interview. Each camera is a self-contained unit. It would take less than a second a piece to slap each one in place if it was prepped with a magnetic strip."

"The press." By the sound of it, Harvey just might kill the whole lot of them. Jim would bet that the President wouldn't complain. "At least we know where the cameraman is now."

Reese was nodding. "One of the press corps. Oh shit!"

"What?"

"I saw..." she squeezed her eyes shut. "Where was I? I saw a stack of small black boxes... Just this size. On a desk."

Her eyes shot open and she grabbed his jacket.

"THE BASEMENT OFFICES underneath the White House Briefing Room." Reese could half see the image.

"What the hell were you doing in there?" They both ignored Harvey.

"Someone working on his camera. I only had a glimpse. I don't know if I even turned in time to see the man's back. Can't even swear it was a man. But I remembered the boxes because I didn't know what they were." Once again she'd missed seeing a person of importance. It was like a gut punch.

"Fine. I'm losing the press vans from the Motorcade. They can scream all they want." Harvey raised his arm to swing his wrist microphone into position, but Jim clamped his hand over Harvey's arm before he could complete the gesture. They looked ready to come to blows.

"Never spook the enemy when you know where they are," Reese had learned that lesson a long time ago. The most misogynistic racers, she always kept them clear in her sights so she'd know the instant they moved in to attack.

"She's right." Again Jim Fischer supporting her, even after dismissing her as a mere fantasy. They *really* needed to talk.

"Besides," Reese agreed, "even if we remove the cameraman, they won't stop the attack."

Harvey glared. "Have you two been drinking the same Kool-Aid?"

Reese looked over at Jim. Their thoughts traveled the same paths so easily. Their bodies had too. How could he...

"Don't you dare get all gooey-eyed on me, Carver," Harvey snapped.

"I wasn't." *She definitely wasn't. She'd sworn to hate Jim Fischer forever, hadn't she? Then why was she still clutching onto his jacket?* She let go—so abruptly that both men noticed it of course.

"We need to just do what we do," Jim spoke fast enough to

show that he too was uneasy. "We trust Reese's abilities to save the President."

"No pressure, huh?"

"Not a bit for a lady like you," and he offered one of his cheery smiles.

She punched him as hard as she could in the solar plexus.

He wasn't the least bit ready for it. Jim gave a long, gasping wheeze, then slowly folded down onto his knees making little *hee-hik* sounds. Malcolm licked his face as a reward.

She turned to Harvey. "I'm *not* getting gooey-eyed over some guy." And she was no man's goddamn fantasy.

Harvey held up both hands and backed up a step, but his smile said that he knew otherwise.

CHAPTER THIRTEEN

*B*y the time Jim got his breath back and wiped the dog slobber off his face, the President's meeting was breaking up.

Again, he barely made it into the Lead Car before the Motorcade rolled out.

Mack and Mark had thought the whole thing was hilarious. Or was it Mark and Mack? They were both classic, six-foot, athletic agents with crew-cut dark hair. And it wasn't just that they looked and sounded alike—he was sure they were swapping names just to mess with him.

The trip to the US Olympic Training Center was almost an exact replay of the trip to the Academy in reverse. Three exits earlier they plunged off I-25 and down onto the city streets. The police had a rolling blockade set up blocks ahead, stopping all side traffic until the Motorcade whisked down East Platte Avenue going eighty miles an hour during what should have been the bumper-to-bumper lunchtime rush hour. The city was going to be a snarl for hours to come—a typical byproduct of a visit by the Presidential Motorcade.

He steered well clear of Reese, even volunteering to augment the local's dog teams. They continued their patrols around the perimeter of the secured site while the President lunched with this year's athletes and his mother—a former medalist and one of the senior swim coaches.

His gut still ached from where she'd caught him, but he wasn't going to rub it and give the guys any more reason to tease him. The entire ride down had been nothing but razzing from the front seat because, of course, every person waiting with the vehicles had witnessed it. He'd seen the blow coming and managed to partially tense for it—though not nearly enough with the power Reese could deliver.

Using Malcolm as an excuse, he left the patrol and grabbed a quick lunch at the Taco Bell on the corner. He had a beef burrito and Malcolm had a tray of diced chicken with cheese— he had a huge weak spot for cheese. One of the servers even gave him a service bowl of water.

Jim was halfway through his meal when Reese walked in with several of the other drivers. It was hard to hide in the crowd when Malcolm picked up her scent and trotted across the restaurant to greet her. Generally, Malcolm was so well behaved that there was no point keeping a leash on him, but he'd grown a definite weak spot where Reese Carver was concerned.

So had Jim.

Reese squatted down to greet Malcolm with a good rub, then looked up at him. After a moment, he could see her sigh deeply before waving Malcolm to return to him.

A minute later, with her plastic tray bearing triple beef tacos, she slid in across from him. He hadn't expected her to join hi—

"Hey, asshole, you okay?"

Or perhaps he did. "Needed to clear all this fresh country

air out of my lungs anyway, I suppose." It earned him a flicker of a smile.

"Not apologizing."

"Figured," he bit into his burrito and ignored Malcolm's pleading eyes. He'd long since finished his chicken and cheese. "Mind telling me what I did?"

"You can't be that stupid." She still wore her sunglasses against the bright Colorado sunlight that poured in through the windows. It made it hard to read what she was thinking.

"Apparently I'm twenty-four cents short of a quarter. Mind explaining? Simple words so a dumb Okie like me can understand?" Not many people made him feel slow, but Reese always raced so far ahead that he was only now beginning to get up to match her speed.

She eyed him for at least half a taco from behind those dark lenses.

He was beginning to wonder if she'd ever speak again when she finally did.

"You called me 'any man's fantasy'."

"No, I called you a goddamn fantasy."

"Well, I'm not."

"You sure are mine."

"Look," she aimed the bit-off end of her second taco at his face like a weapon. "I'm not some fantasy poster on a stupid-ass garage calendar."

"Shit! Is that what you thought I meant?" He could see how that might piss her off.

"Isn't it?" Reese was clearly aiming for scoff, but fouled that ball off into still-seething anger.

"Reese. I never even dreamed of being with a woman like you."

She opened her mouth to protest.

"And no, I'm not talking about your looks—which are

incredible—or your body—which is awesome. I'm talking about *you*. I drove for a living from the moment I got my license to the day I got Malcolm. I know enough to *see* what you can do. What you did putting the Beast through its paces out at James J. Rowley Training Center. What you did to save the First Lady. No matter what you say, that isn't 'I just drive.' It was a goddamn miracle to watch. I *know* what that takes to do. I sure as hell couldn't have pulled it off. Ralph McKenna couldn't. You stunned him speechless out at RTC. Tell me what part of that doesn't fit fantasy woman."

"The part that makes *me* a fantasy girl," but this time she didn't make it an accusation. This time there was some humor and maybe a bit of surprise.

"Well, shit, woman," he leaned back and did his best to match her suddenly nonchalant tone. "Gonna have to get used to it if you're gonna hang around this ol' boy."

They ate in what he hoped was companionable silence until "Ten minutes!" squawked over their radios. They drained their sodas and hustled out the door as fast as the snarl of rushing agents allowed.

REESE HAD a lot to think about after they checked over the vehicles once more and she locked and strapped herself in.

Maybe the way Jim had actually meant it, being a fantasy woman didn't sound all bad.

Though she still wrestled with being more than a 'just a driver.' Granted, she wouldn't be sitting in this seat if that's all she was. But when she looked out the sideview mirrors and saw the rest of the vehicles arrayed around her, she felt very small.

When the President climbed aboard and called out his

friendly greeting, she managed to respond. Secretary Matthews and Franks Adams followed him in, then Harvey closed the heavy door, which weighed as much as the door on a Boeing 757—over three hundred pounds—and hustled around to his own door.

Out the windshield, she saw Jim scramble into the back of the Lead Car. He turned around to smile at her and wave as Harvey buckled himself in.

"That boy is gone on you, Carver."

"Yes, sir." There was no denying it. And after his amazing speech, in a Taco Bell of all bizarre places, she was starting to feel a little gone on him.

A little gone on him?

Not even close. She finally understood that she'd crossed that line a long time ago. He saw her in ways that she certainly didn't see herself. As if she was somehow amazing. And he was forcing her, inch by grudging inch, to see those parts of herself.

The Lead Car moved out.

She could hear the President and Secretary of State Matthews in the back of the car. Every spare minute they'd been talking about some country or other. She'd only caught snippets: South China Sea security, Indo-Russian Zapad military exercise, Egyptian government. They sat at the far back and were hard to hear even though they left the glass partition down. Chief of Staff Cornelia Day, who sat in the rear-facing seat directly behind Reese's own, spoke rarely but the two men always listened when she did.

"We leaving anytime soon?" Harvey teased her.

Reese dropped into gear and quickly closed the four-car-length gap that she'd let open up between her and the Lead Car.

Out of the parking lot, down a quiet wooded block, and a left onto East Platte Avenue. The four-lane major thoroughfare was already closed eastbound for the short seven-mile run to Peterson Air Force Base and the waiting Air Force One. The President would make the short hop to Buckley Air Force Base outside of Denver, then hold onboard meetings while the Motorcade raced the ninety miles north to rejoin him. The next sortie for the Motorcade wouldn't be until the dinnertime fundraiser and they'd be there hours ahead of that.

Through the narrow congestion of the first few blocks, there was little to see except for the bare limbs of the tall maple trees. Dark clouds were building to the West and the bright sun in the blue eastern sky was getting squeezed out fast.

Then they fell off the edge. What little beauty existed in Colorado Springs—arid landscape just didn't sit right for a woman from the South—decayed into a depressingly familiar strip of light industrial and mini-mall sprawl.

On the plus side, the east and west lanes became broader and were separated by a low curb. The intersections were farther apart and the Motorcade began moving up to its normal speed. They were soon headed east at eighty miles an hour, little more than a long black blur to the people lining the roadside with their cell phone cameras.

She began counting down the miles like minutes: six to go, five, four.

A feeling of complacency that she recognized from her days of racing settled over her.

Stay in the slot and ride the groove home.

There was one key lesson she'd learned about that particular feeling—it was almost invariably wrong!

"Shit!" Reese raised her voice, "Everyone in back. Check your seatbelts." She heard two loud snaps. Complacency! Double shit!

Harvey looked at her in surprise.

"Hang on!" She couldn't see it coming—whatever *it* was.

But she could feel it.

JIM WATCHED the Pilot Car and the motorcycle sweepers flash through the closed intersection ahead, against the red light. Things like red lights had no bearing on the Motorcade.

They were passing the last big box stores. Over the rise he could see the first ramped exit as East Platt Avenue transitioned into the divided State Highway 24. That exit and one more would see them safely back onto Peterson Air Force Base.

Other than a Perkins pancake restaurant and a pawn shop, they were out of town.

"Looks like an armored car convention," Mack spoke up from the driver's seat. Jim had finally straightened out which of them was which. Mark rode shotgun, literally—with the weapon propped between his feet.

Jim looked between the front seats and out the windshield. On the far side of the intersection, eight armored cars—the heavy-duty ones that banks used to move cash—were parked four on each side of East Platte Avenue.

He didn't even need to think.

"Turn right!" Eight armored cars weren't a convention. They were the attack!

"Why?" But Mack slammed into a sideways skid before he even finished asking the question. The motorcycle cop who'd been stopping traffic at the intersection barely had time to dive away from his bike before they slammed into it sideways. The collision was enough to get them headed south on whatever road this was.

Jim pinned Malcolm to the floor under his legs and glanced back along East Platte. He saw the armored trucks already in motion off the sides of the road, plowing into the police escort.

Cop cars, motorcycles, and—he swallowed hard—bodies were scattered in every direction.

Twisting further, he saw that Reese had taken the turn better than they had, doing her job of sticking on the Lead Car's tail.

"Two more!" Mack called out.

At the end of the block, two of the big trucks were already rolling off the curb to block their escape. The attackers had anticipated this possible escape route. Did they have access to the alternate route plan, or was it simply good logistics? Either way, at the moment it was working.

Jim struggled to remember. The road to the left was called something Loop. Loop was a bad sign.

"Right again!" There weren't any other choices.

The Lead Car slewed onto the narrow two-lane road—lights and siren blaring.

Two leafless maples stood by the Pine Tree Square road sign. They blasted by a dry cleaners.

"What have you gotten us into, Fischer?"

"Damned if I know, Mack. Just don't slow down." They were on a very narrow two-lane lined with trees and a sidewalk.

"No shit, Sherlock."

Jim twisted to watch behind while Mack drove ahead.

Reese had managed the turn and was tight on their tail.

One of the Spares stopped sideways across the entry to the road, spanning all the way across the entrance.

An armored truck slammed into it at speed, plowing into it so hard that the truck's rear end lifted at least five feet off the ground. The Spare was blasted aside in a tumbling roll. The hit was hard enough to crumple the armored truck's front end.

Goliath versus Goliath, both had lost. But three more trucks raced into the breach their companion had made.

He keyed the mic. "They're pros, Reese. Serious pros."

There was no response, but their gazes met across the tiny gap that separated their vehicles. She gave him a sharp nod of acknowledgement.

Halfback came in behind. Revealing its true colors, the Suburban's split roof had been flipped open and an M134 Minigun had popped up. These trucks would be armored to B7 standards, able to survive a hit from a 7.62x51mm round. But the four thousand rounds a minute that the M134 could deliver was another matter. Despite the roaring engines, Jim could hear the distinct, chainsaw *Brap!* of the gun as it tore at the armored trucks.

He prayed for no stray rounds. The Beast could take it, far better than the armored trucks, but he was in a production Chevy Impala. Not so much!

"WE'VE STILL GOT HALFBACK," Harvey reported.

Reese had seen the Spare take the hit for her. Even inside the Beast's armor, the driver would be lucky to live through that blow.

"Where's the rest of the Motorcade?" President Thomas shouted from the back.

"Doesn't matter," she and Harvey yelled in unison. Harvey got the "sir" on the end—she didn't.

Whether the rest of the Motorcade was in the fight of their lives or quietly parked on East Platte Avenue didn't matter to her—they weren't here. That was all that counted.

The Lead Car twisted left, then right through a short-sharp S that was meant to be taken at ten miles an hour, not sixty. In another hundred meters it opened onto a large parking lot—if she could get that far. The lead armored truck managed to tap her rear bumper, but she didn't have any weapons back there big enough to stop them. She needed a missile.

As if in answer, a missile slammed down from above.

Overwatch—the Black Hawk helicopter that always flew above the Motorcade. Such a fixture that she never gave it any thought.

The third armored car disintegrated.

Halfback had been chasing so closely that they slammed into the wreckage. The Protection Detail poured out the doors of the destroyed vehicle even as it burned.

Now it was just her and Jim's Lead Car against the two remaining armoreds.

She had half a second to understand what she'd just done. It wasn't the *Lead Car* anymore. It was Jim himself who had seen and understood what was happening. *He* was the one protecting her and the President. Without him, they'd probably be dead on East Platte Avenue by now. He understood driving *and* battle.

Reese was willing to trust her life to his hands. And rather than being afraid, it gave her a renewed confidence.

In her rearview, she almost missed the streak of light slicing upward from the back of the second armored vehicle.

JIM COULD ONLY WATCH in horror as the RPG shot upward from the rear of the second armored vehicle.

Overwatch, which had moved in for the kill, never stood a chance of evading.

They did manage to get the second missile off but it went

astray and punched a smoking crater among the vehicles of the nearby parking lot.

The helo twisted and spun, tumbling out of the sky. Whether it was by chance or plan—it was hard to tell—the helo slammed into the second armored truck and both disappeared in a ball of fire.

"And then there was one," he whispered to himself.

"You wish," Mack didn't sound happy.

Jim spun around. They'd emerged into a vast parking lot. Some people were running, others were just gawking.

The long, low stretch of a super-sized Walmart store rose before them.

"Don't go around the side! It's one lane. Too easy to trap us there."

Mack slewed them into the frontage road along the front of the building. It was crammed with people. People, and two more armored trucks that must have come in from the original group on East Platte Avenue. He continued the turn and raced into the depths of the parking lot.

Someone lost their shopping cart and Mack slammed it aside. Jim half expected a squeaky toy moment on the windshield. Instead, big Number 10 cans of tomato sauce slammed into the Impala like mortars. One shattered the right side of the windshield as it shredded and they were all covered with tomato sauce. He'd have preferred the squeaky toy.

"Thanks, Mack," Mark must be okay to be complaining in that steady tone.

"Needed a shower anyway, Mark." Mack was fast running out of parking lot.

The other two armoreds were moving to block exits.

Jim had an idea. "Take us back, Mack. Straight at the main entrance."

"Wish someone here knew what they were doing, because it sure doesn't sound like you," but he did it anyway.

"Just gun it for all you're worth."

Jim spun around to face Reese, who was still right on their tail. They had outrun the armored truck by twenty yards and the gap was growing.

He spun his finger in the air and then jabbed a finger forward as if she was launching gas canisters from a spinning car. He could only hope she understood.

"You've got a radio, doofus," her voice sounded in his earpiece, "but I get it. How badly are you hurt?"

"Hurt?" Then some more sauce dripped out of his hair. "Tomato sauce. We're going to go left."

He saw her nod of understanding.

REESE RACED after the Lead Car, then braced herself. She'd only done this once and that had been on a quiet practice field. No narrow lines of parked cars. No people running away, screaming.

At least the people inside her car weren't screaming. Instead, a grim silence had settled over them while they waited for Reese to save them.

Some idiot started to back her Ford Fiesta out of a spot.

The Lead Car managed to swerve clear, but the Beast clipped the car hard. It spun away, bounced off a few others before Reese had raced by. The armored truck blew through it like it was week-old Kleenex.

Jim's car, as he promised, turned left, then left again, racing once more into the depths of the parking lot.

Reese started her spin as she exited the parking lane. In the broad pick-up/drop-off area in front of the store, she managed to get through her one-eighty. Harvey fired the tear gas canisters for her at exactly the right moment.

She let the spin continue but there wasn't enough room.

The side of the Beast slammed sideways into the four, six-inch concrete pillars that guarded the entrance. Three of them snapped off, but it stopped her sideways momentum. There was a hard thump and a sharp cry from the back. Perfect, she'd probably just concussed the President against the inside of a five-inch thick car window.

The Kevlar tires got traction and they shot aside mere moments before the armored truck came racing out of the cloud of tear gas. Braking too late, it flew past the pillars and disappeared through the front entrance of the Walmart in a cloud of glass shards and metal doorframes.

Gunning it for all she was worth, she headed deep into the parking lot once more.

She saw figures in black running in from East Platte Avenue.

The Counter Assault Team. There was blood on some faces. One ran with one arm hanging limp at his side and a rifle in his other hand.

In moments, one of the CAT unleashed an RPG. The rocket-propelled grenade raced across the Walmart parking lot toward one of the waiting armored cars. The grenade seemed to think about it for a moment after it hit beneath the lower edge of the driver's door. For a moment she thought it was miss. Then the explosion bloomed upward, lifting the truck and knocking it onto its side. The shot had been intentionally low for that purpose.

A second RPG, that must have been fired before the first one even hit, slammed straight into the now-exposed gas tank, and the truck disappeared in a ball of flame. Now that was *her* kind of teamwork.

The last armored truck was trying to make good its escape, racing along the front of the store.

Reese ran a long curve through gaps in the middle of the parking lot, then chose her lane.

"What are you doing?" Harvey shouted from the right hand seat where he'd been trying to coordinate all of the attacks and counterattacks.

Yes, it was her job to get the protectees to safety. It was supposed to be her only job. But she had another idea.

"Get him!" President Thomas shouted from the back.

Precisely! She was sick to death of people ramming her, battering her, trying to beat her down when she was just trying to run the race.

Well, not this time.

In her lane, she raced the Beast back toward the building.

Maybe the armored truck didn't see her coming.

Jim had the Lead Car racing along in front of it. He'd punched out the back window and was firing round after round into the armored truck's windshield with a shotgun. The armored's windshield was tougher than that, but it was likely badly star-cracked.

She slammed into the side of the armored car at over thirty miles an hour.

It flew sideways into the massive block-concrete wall of the Walmart and disappeared inside the store.

Reese backed up, ready to ram it again.

Harvey rested a hand on her arm, "Enough. They're out of the contest."

Reese glanced out her side window.

The Lead Car sat there, not ten feet away. Jim and Malcolm were grinning at her as Jim held his shotgun aimed at the sky. She could see the red sauce still matted in his hair.

It was easy to grin back.

Then the Lead Car pulled away and she turned to follow. She could feel that her Beast was limping. The hood was twisted up, the status indicator showed that three of the four tires had been blown and she was running on the inner tread. But she was running.

They covered the last two miles to the airport slowly, with no Motorcade, but they delivered a healthy President and Chief of Staff to Air Force One. Secretary Matthews would be wearing an arm cast for a while. Frank Adams nearly carried him aboard they were moving up the stairs so fast.

The blue-and-white plane already had its engines running and was in the air before she had a chance to park the Beast out of the way.

CHAPTER FOURTEEN

*R*eese sat wide awake in the silent darkness trying to understand what was happening to her and how she'd come to be here.

Jim lay asleep with his head on her lap; he had a hand wrapped lazily over her bare thigh. Her hand was tangled in his hair, which was almost as soft as Malcolm's, who lay upon her feet. She was warmed by two males...*her* two males.

It was an uncomfortable thought for such a comfortable position.

A comfortable position in...

She sighed, softly, so as not to wake her boys.

She'd often been asked about the possibilities of sex in a stock car—invariably in the crudest of ways. And the answer was that it was wholly impossible. A stock car had a single bucket seat wrapped in a steel roll cage. Steering wheel, stick shift, and protective padding turned it from seat into cocoon for one. It was not a place for claustrophobes.

Not that she'd disliked the image, just the jerks who tried to use it as an opening line. Sex in a hot racing car. Two very good things in the same space.

She'd never thought to have sex in their current location however.

She, Jim, and Malcolm were on the homebound leg back to Andrews Air Force Base in the guts of a C-17 Globemaster III jet transport. The Beast limousine had been loaded aboard with the three other surviving vehicles from the Motorcade—there'd been eight aboard on the way out. Air Force One and the President were already safely back in DC; the Marine One helicopter seeing to the final stage of returning the President safely to the White House.

They'd been over Kansas when Malcolm had come up to her sitting in one of the forward crew area seats. The other drivers with her were either fast asleep in their seats or involved in an intense game of poker. The C-17's crew were sitting up forward with the pilots.

She and Jim were the only other ones awake…except that she didn't see Jim anywhere.

Malcolm appeared anxious to return to his master, so she waved him away and, after only a moment's consideration, followed the dog. He'd led her past the first three vehicles in the massive cargo bay only barely lit with red nightlights. Just enough light so that she didn't trip over the front-and-rear chains anchoring each vehicle to the deck so that they couldn't shift in flight.

At the rear of the aircraft had sat the battered Beast. Her car.

And the massive rear door had been propped open, ever so slightly.

She'd hesitated again, longer that time. It hadn't been difficult to guess what awaited her—a truly amazing man—but the implications were huge!

To make love with Jim Fischer in the back of *her* car was part teenage fantasy. But that car was also all that she was.

No. She'd only *thought* it was all she was. Jim had proved to her that she was more than just the car she drove. She was also a woman that he wanted to survive—the one he believed in so deeply.

That had been enough to have her pulling open the door, allowing Malcolm to climb in where he curled up on the President's seat.

Then she'd stepped in herself to join the man waiting for her.

She hadn't been convinced that it was the right choice, but she'd stepped in anyway and pulled the door shut.

And now, despite what they'd just done, she still wasn't.

The question was, did she want to be convinced?

Inside the Beast, the outer world had gone away. The tinted windows dark enough to allow only the softest glow from the plane's red nightlights to filter into the car. The heavy armor cut off the massive roar of the four big Pratt & Whitney engines, and her ears had popped when she removed her earplugs.

Initially they'd simply sat on the forward bench talking about the car, the Motorcade, and their narrow escape from the attack.

The reporter, a long brunette, had put on a real show of horror at the whole situation, even as she was caught recovering a camera from the bottom of the flipped and destroyed Spare—though the driver had gotten off with only a broken wrist.

She'd been promised Pulitzer material and a million-dollar bonus to keep her mouth shut about how she got the images. She'd signaled her accomplice the moment the First Lady's

Motorcade had left the UN, and the instant that the President's Motorcade had left the Olympic Training Center.

The other side of the chain had been less obvious until she finally revealed that she was sleeping with a Saudi prince from a renegade branch of the royal family. Or at least that's what they were calling it now. Who knew the actual truth. The prince in question had regrettably died during "an accident" shortly after his arrest. The king had promised more answers soon.

The Beast's armor made the car so well insulated that their own body heat soon had them opening, then peeling off their jackets.

She remembered how Jim's smile had made peeling off her blouse seem so natural just moments later. Any residual hints of chill had been scorched away by the attention he'd lavished upon her willing body.

It was only as they were deep in the throes of their encounter that she began to *appreciate* the location.

They were in the Beast.

They were in *her* car!

A charge had run through her as that insight fought its way through the blinding heat that Jim had generated to replace the last of the cold. It didn't take long before they'd fogged the windows.

"It's like the mile-high club, only better," Jim had whispered close by her ear.

"We were over a mile high in the Colorado Springs parking lot," she'd teased.

Being made love to in the Beast, inside an airplane, while flying six miles up in the sky should have been the upper limit. But Jim had found a way to pack the power of turbo-charged adrenaline rush into a moment of such gentle perfection that the explosion of their bodies should have launched them into orbit.

Thankfully sound traveled no better out of the Beast than it did inward, because the cry that burst from her was unstoppable. She'd never felt anything like the joy that Jim had pumped into her body as she'd knelt over him in the deep leather seat, her hands braced on the ceiling, his hands firmly clamped about her waist and his face buried between her breasts.

Would it last?

When she'd finally come down, when she had at long last managed to flop bonelessly into the seat beside him and he'd laid his head in her lap, she could finally ask the question.

But the question, she now knew, was pointless.

She *knew* it would last. The pleasure they gave each other might someday become familiar, but she suspected that too would always be exceptional. The least experience with Jim far overshadowed the best moment of anything prior.

But even that truly didn't matter.

Jim didn't just want sex with her. Neither did he want to change her into someone she wasn't. He would always be the patient, even-tempered person in their relationship. And she would always be the quiet one who had to be coaxed into facing anything inside her.

Inside her.

She could feel Jim inside her. And from far more than the delicious sex.

She could feel him inside her like a light. Like the green flag fluttering high above the track the moment before it flashed downward to launch the cars on their way.

He believed in her. Not merely her ability to drive, but also her ability to make the right decision in crisis. He stood inside her with a purity of faith as clear as her father's had been. Perhaps more so.

Her father had never seen past the next race, the next season. All he'd focused on was the edge of the envelope...and it had killed him. There was more than the next race. There was more than the points-ranking for the season.

Reese hadn't understood that before.

Yet Jim always saw all of the futures ahead of them.

She brushed her hand through his hair and listened to his sleeping breath. Yes, he'd showed her how to see more than the next time at the wheel. He'd taught her how to believe in a future she'd never even given thought to—never mind dreamed about or believed in.

And still her beautiful man slept in her lap in the back seat of *her* car.

She wiggled her toes under Malcolm.

He at least woke up enough to sigh happily.

Jim slept on, unaware of the change he'd made inside Reese's heart.

It was okay. He'd have years and years to learn about those changes.

So would she.

EPILOGUE

*J*im stood on the broad white marble step at the west end of the White House Rose Garden amid the June roses.

Malcolm stood by his side; his coat brushed until he shone in the bright sun.

Captain Baxter stood by his shoulder as best man. "Got you through the Uniformed Division. Least I can do is get you through a damned wedding without you screwing it up."

Ralph McKenna had flown in from retirement in Washington State for the wedding and to walk Reese up the aisle, then had to fight Harvey Lieber for the privilege. Last Jim had heard they were both going to walk her down the aisle.

Seated across the Rose Garden lawn were K-9 members and Motorcade drivers as well as the President, senior advisors, and all of his own family—their big rigs were parked out at his place.

Out at his *and* Reese's place.

Their home.

She'd gotten shaky when he gave her a key to the place,

which had given him an idea. For his wedding present, he had signed half of the property's deed over to her because he wanted her to have a real home again.

Reese had cried so hard that he'd considered calling 9-1-1 before she finally recovered. *Together,* she'd promised. Together they would build a house there someday. A house with an extra bedroom for a child. She hadn't argued when he'd insisted that it would also have a shower big enough for two.

Instead, they'd had wedding eve sex that was so gentle and so perfect that *he'd* almost cried.

Secretary Matthews stood there beside him as he'd be performing the ceremony.

"You've got your flag?" Jim whispered to him.

"I do. That was an excellent idea." He pointed behind the potted rose tree that defined one side of the altar. The furled black-and-white checkered flag—the exact same brand and size waved for winning a NASCAR race—was ready for Secretary Matthews to flourish over their heads when Jim kissed the bride. President Thomas had given him special permission to replace the standard Sunoco gas emblem in the middle with the Presidential Seal.

He heard the soft rumble of the big diesel engine only moments before her car pulled into sight. Eighteen feet of shining black, armored Beast rolled along the driveway that encircled the south lawn and stopped by the garden entrance near the South Portico.

Dilya climbed out of the front passenger seat—Reese's bridesmaid. Dilya had been horribly frustrated, trying to fit them into her whole *Pride and Prejudice* storyline. He'd never been prejudiced and being prideful was not a problem for Reese. Getting her to acknowledge her own worth and value was the challenge—though why such an amazing woman had so much trouble seeing it was beyond him. While she'd gotten better about it over the last several months, she would never understand how truly incredible she was. But that was okay—he did.

Jim was watching the back passenger door and completely missed the moment when the driver's door on the far side swung open and Reese stepped out of the car.

His laugh was first, but only by moments—the rest of the wedding party caught on quickly.

Harvey Lieber and Ralph McKenna exited from the rear doors.

Because, of course, Reese Carver drove the limousine to her own wedding.

The laughter died like an eighteen-wheel blowout as she stepped around the car into clear view.

Reese Carver was a vision.

Her long black hair fell behind her shoulders in a single shining wave. She wore a dress of white lace. It was off the shoulder, with a low collar that revealed her lovely neck and collarbone. The long-sleeved, open-patterned, white lace down her arms was backed by the warm, dark luster of her skin. The dress clung to her curves, the lace spilling past where the lining ended at mid-thigh to once again tease with more hints of her skin until her athlete's legs were ultimately revealed by the scalloped hem.

"You lucky shit!" Dad whispered from where he stood at the first row of seats.

Mom elbowed him, but since she was busy dabbing at her eyes with a tissue, there wasn't much force behind it.

Some White House lady photographer with long silver hair moved in to take photos.

Dilya led the way in a dress that made her look far more like a graceful young adult than a precocious kid almost grown. Someday, she was going to make some guy seriously happy…and keep him seriously challenged.

But it was only Reese that he could see walking toward him.

Malcolm trotted down the aisle to join Reese, then turned to walk back with her—nearly causing Harvey Lieber to go down.

Jim could see his mouth move as he swore silently.

But none of that mattered.

All that mattered was that the distance between Reese and himself was closing with each passing second. Soon they would cross the finish line together and *that* win would last them a lifetime.

OFF THE LEASH (EXCERPT)

IF YOU MISSED LINDA AND CLIVE, BUY IT NOW!

Look for *In the Weeds* coming soon!

OFF THE LEASH (EXCERPT)

"*Y*ou're joking."

"Nope. That's his name. And he's yours now."

Sergeant Linda Hamlin wondered quite what it would take to wipe that smile off Lieutenant Jurgen's face. A 120mm round from an M1A1 Abrams Main Battle Tank came to mind.

The kennel master of the US Secret Service's Canine Team was clearly a misogynistic jerk from the top of his polished head to the bottoms of his equally polished boots. She wondered if the shoelaces were polished as well.

Then she looked over at the poor dog sitting hopefully on the concrete kennel floor. His stall had a dog bed three times his size and a water bowl deep enough for him to bathe in. No toys, because toys always came from the handler as a reward. He offered her a sad sigh and a liquid doggy gaze. The kennel even smelled wrong, more of sanitizer than dog. The walls seemed to echo with each bark down the long line of kennels housing the candidate hopefuls for the next addition to the Secret Service's team.

Thor—really?—was a brindle-colored mutt, part who-knew and part no-one-cared. He looked like a cross between an oversized, long-haired schnauzer and a dust mop that someone had spilled dark gray paint on. After mixing in streaks of tawny brown, they'd left one white paw just to make him all the more laughable.

And of course Lieutenant Jerk Jurgen would assign Thor to the first woman on the USSS K-9 team.

Unable to resist, she leaned over far enough to scruff the dog's ears. He was the physical opposite of the sleek and powerful Malinois MWDs—military war dogs—that she'd been handling for the 75th Rangers for the last five years. They twitched with eagerness and nerves. A good MWD was seventy pounds of pure drive—every damn second of the day. If the mild-mannered Thor weighed thirty pounds, she'd be surprised. And he looked like a little girl's best friend who should have a pink bow on his collar.

Jurgen was clearly ex-Marine and would have no respect for the Army. Of course, having been in the Army's Special Operations Forces, she knew better than to respect a Marine.

"We won't let any old swabbie bother us, will we?"

Jurgen snarled—definitely Marine Corps. Swabbie was slang for a Navy sailor and a Marine always took offense at being lumped in with them no matter how much they belonged. Of course the swabbies took offense at having the Marines lumped with *them*. Too bad there weren't any Navy around so that she could get two for the price of one. Jurgen wouldn't be her boss, so appeasing him wasn't high on her to-do list.

At least she wouldn't need any of the protective bite gear working with Thor. With his stature, he was an explosives detection dog without also being an attack one.

"Where was he trained?" She stood back up to face the beast.

"Private outfit in Montana—some place called Henderson's Ranch. Didn't make their MWD program," his scoff said exactly what he thought the likelihood of any dog outfit in Montana being worthwhile. "They wanted us to try the little runt out."

She'd never heard of a training program in Montana. MWDs all came out of Lackland Air Force Base training. The Secret Service mostly trained their own and they all came from Vohne Liche Kennels in Indiana. Unless... Special Operations Forces dogs were trained by private contractors. She'd worked beside a Delta Force dog for a single month—he'd been incredible.

"Is he trained in English or German?" Most American MWDs were trained in German so that there was no confusion in case a command word happened to be part of a spoken sentence. It also made it harder for any random person on the battlefield to shout something that would confuse the dog.

"German according to his paperwork, but he won't listen to me much in either language."

Might as well give the diminutive Thor a few basic tests. A snap of her fingers and a slap on her thigh had the dog dropping into a smart "heel" position. No need to call out *Fuss* —*by my foot.*

"*Pass auf!*" *Guard!* She made a pistol with her thumb and forefinger and aimed it at Jurgen as she grabbed her forearm with her other hand—the military hand sign for enemy.

The little dog snarled at Jurgen sharply enough to have him backing out of the kennel. "Goddamn it!"

"*Ruhig.*" *Quiet.* Thor maintained his fierce posture but dropped the snarl.

"*Gute Hund.*" *Good dog,* Linda countered the command.

Thor looked up at her and wagged his tail happily. She tossed him a doggie treat, which he caught midair and crunched happily.

She didn't bother looking up at Jurgen as she knelt once more to check over the little dog. His scruffy fur was so soft that it tickled. Good strength in the jaw, enough to show he'd had bite training despite his size—perfect if she ever needed to take down a three-foot-tall terrorist. Legs said he was a jumper.

"Take your time, Hamlin. I've got nothing else to do with the rest of my goddamn day except babysit you and this mutt."

"Is the course set?"

"Sure. Take him out," Jurgen's snarl sounded almost as nasty as Thor's before he stalked off.

She stood and slapped a hand on her opposite shoulder.

Thor sprang aloft as if he was attached to springs and she caught him easily. He'd cleared well over double his own height. Definitely trained…and far easier to catch than seventy pounds of hyperactive Malinois.

She plopped him back down on the ground. On lead or off? She'd give him the benefit of the doubt and try off first to see what happened.

Linda zipped up her brand-new USSS jacket against the cold and led the way out of the kennel into the hard sunlight of the January morning. Snow had brushed the higher hills around the USSS James J. Rowley Training Center—which this close to Washington, DC, wasn't saying much—but was melting quickly. Scents wouldn't carry as well on the cool air, making it more of a challenge for Thor to locate the explosives. She didn't know where they were either. The course was a test for handler as well as dog.

Jurgen would be up in the observer turret looking for any

excuse to mark down his newest team. Perhaps teasing him about being just a Marine hadn't been her best tactical choice. She sighed. At least she was consistent—she'd always been good at finding ways to piss people off before she could stop herself and consider the wisdom of doing so.

This test was the culmination of a crazy three months, so she'd forgive herself this time—something she also wasn't very good at.

In October she'd been out of the Army and unsure what to do next. Tucked in the packet with her DD 214 honorable discharge form had been a flyer on career opportunities with the US Secret Service dog team: *Be all your dog can be!* No one else being released from Fort Benning that day had received any kind of a job flyer at all that she'd seen, so she kept quiet about it.

She had to pass through DC on her way back to Vermont—her parent's place. Burlington would work for, honestly, not very long at all, but she lacked anywhere else to go after a decade of service. So, she'd stopped off in DC to see what was up with that job flyer. Five interviews and three months to complete a standard six-month training course later—which was mostly a cakewalk after fighting with the US Rangers—she was on-board and this chill January day was her first chance with a dog. First chance to prove that she still had it. First chance to prove that she hadn't made a mistake in deciding that she'd seen enough bloodshed and war zones for one lifetime and leaving the Army.

The Start Here sign made it obvious where to begin, but she didn't dare hesitate to take in her surroundings past a quick glimpse. Jurgen's score would count a great deal toward where she and Thor were assigned in the future. Mostly likely on some field prep team, clearing the way for presidential visits.

As usual, hindsight informed her that harassing the lieutenant hadn't been an optimal strategy. A hindsight that had served her equally poorly with regular Army commanders before she'd finally hooked up with the Rangers—kowtowing to officers had never been one of her strengths.

Thankfully, the Special Operations Forces hadn't given a damn about anything except performance and *that* she could always deliver, since the day she'd been named the team captain for both soccer and volleyball. She was never popular, but both teams had made all-state her last two years in school.

The canine training course at James J. Rowley was a two-acre lot. A hard-packed path of tramped-down dirt led through the brown grass. It followed a predictable pattern from the gate to a junker car, over to tool shed, then a truck, and so on into a compressed version of an intersection in a small town. Beyond it ran an urban street of gray clapboard two- and three-story buildings and an eight-story office tower, all without windows. Clearly a playground for Secret Service training teams.

Her target was the town, so she blocked the city street out of her mind. Focus on the problem: two roads, twenty storefronts, six houses, vehicles, pedestrians.

It might look normal...normalish with its missing windows and no movement. It would be anything but. Stocked with fake IEDs, a bombmaker's stash, suicide cars, weapons caches, and dozens of other traps, all waiting for her and Thor to find. He had to be sensitive to hundreds of scents and it was her job to guide him so that he didn't miss the opportunity to find and evaluate each one.

There would be easy scents, from fertilizer and diesel fuel used so destructively in the 1995 Oklahoma City bombing, to almost as obvious TNT to the very difficult to detect C-4 plastic explosive.

Mannequins on the street carried grocery bags and briefcases. Some held fresh meat, a powerful smell demanding any dog's attention, but would count as a false lead if they went for it. On the job, an explosives detection dog wasn't supposed to care about anything except explosives. Other mannequins were wrapped in suicide vests loaded with Semtex or wearing knapsacks filled with package bombs made from Russian PVV-5A.

She spotted Jurgen stepping into a glassed-in observer turret atop the corner drugstore. Someone else was already there and watching.

She looked down once more at the ridiculous little dog and could only hope for the best.

"Thor?"

He looked up at her.

She pointed to the left, away from the beaten path.

"Such!" Find.

Thor sniffed left, then right. Then he headed forward quickly in the direction she pointed.

CLIVE ANDREWS SAT in the second-story window at the corner of Main and First, the only two streets in town. Downstairs was a drugstore all rigged to explode, except there were no triggers and there was barely enough explosive to blow up a candy box.

Not that he'd know, but that's what Lieutenant Jurgen had promised him.

It didn't really matter if it was rigged to blow for real, because when Miss Watson—never Ms. or Mrs.—asked for a "favor," you did it. At least he did. Actually, he had yet to meet anyone else who knew her. Not that he'd asked around. She wasn't the sort of person one talked about with strangers, or even close friends. He'd bet even if they did, it would be in whispers. That's just what she was like.

So he'd traveled across town from the White House and into Maryland on a cold winter's morning, barely past a sunrise that did nothing to warm the day. Now he sat in an unheated glass icebox and watched a new officer run a test course he didn't begin to understand. Lieutenant Jurgen settled in beside him at a console with feeds from a dozen cameras and banks of switches.

While waiting, Clive had been fooling around with a sketch on a small pad of paper. The next State Dinner was in seven days. President Zachary Taylor had invited the leaders of Vietnam, Japan, and the Philippines to the White House for discussions about some Chinese islands. Or something like that, Clive hadn't really been paying attention to the details past the attendee list.

Instead, he was contemplating the dessert for such a dinner that would surprise, perhaps delight, as well as being an icebreaker for future discussions. Being the chocolatier for the White House was the most exciting job he'd ever had. Every challenge was fresh and new, like the first strawberry of each year.

This one would be elegant. January was a little early, it would be better if it was spring, but that wasn't crucial. A large half-egg shape of paper-thin white chocolate filled with a mousse—white chocolate? No, nor a dark chocolate. Instead, a milk chocolate mousse but rich with flavor, perhaps bourbon. Then mold the dark chocolate to top it with a filigree bird, wings spread in half flight, ready to soar upward. A crane perhaps? He made a note to check with the protocol office to make sure that he wouldn't be offending some leader without knowing it.

"Never underestimate the power of a good dessert," he mumbled one of Jacques Torres' favorite admonitions. This was going to work very nicely.

"What's that?" Jurgen grunted out without looking up.

"Just talking to myself."

Which earned him a dismissive grunt, as if he was unworthy of the agent's attention. It wouldn't surprise him. Clive was not trained like a Secret Service officer. His skills lay in his palate and his fingers for shaping the very finest chocolate work. He knew his big frame and good looks said easy-going and, while his size wasn't quite to oaf, people always assumed he was just a big and clumsy guy.

Clive often felt defensive about being a chocolatier when he was so dismissed out of hand. He had spent years learning his skills. And to be invited to join the White House kitchen...well, he couldn't think of a higher accolade. The fact that his father would agree with Jurgen didn't help matters. However, Lieutenant Jurgen didn't look like the sort of man to risk upsetting.

His own father had been a quiet, drunken merchant marine who rarely spoke when he was ashore—except for grumblings about his only child's lame excuse for a choice of profession. The one blessing of having Nic Andrews as a father was how much of Clive's life the man had spent at sea. In between, Clive and his mother had lived together in Redwood City very quietly and with some small degree of content. Their apartment had a view of the brilliant colors of the Cargill Salt Flats of San Francisco Bay. He often used their colors in his chocolates.

"They're starting." It was clear by his tone that Jurgen could break Clive over his knee like a piece of sugar work despite Clive's size and would be glad to demonstrate at the least provocation.

"Oh, thanks," seemed to be an acceptable response.

A "you're welcome" grunt sounded softly.

Miss Watson had told him to watch, so he closed his notepad and tucked it in his shirt pocket.

"Any suggestions on what I'm looking for?" Miss Watson had *not* been clear on that point. He looked down at the new officer and the small dog entering the far end of the course. He picked up a pair of binoculars from the window ledge but the dog was still small, barely reaching the officer's knees.

He scanned upward.

A woman. For some reason he hadn't expected that. Of course with the silly little dog, that somehow fit. However, officer or not, the woman offered a great deal to be looking at. Five-seven or eight. Medium chocolate brunette, about a fifty percent cocoa, with a nicely tempered shine like a fine ganache. It fell in a natural flow down to her shoulders, slightly ragged rather than in some DC socialite perfect coif. A thin face without being gaunt. Perhaps intense would be a better word.

Her jacket hid her shape, but she wore no hat or gloves despite the cold. Tan khakis hinted at nice legs. Army boots declared definitely not DC socialite.

"Well, for one thing, she's not following the damned course," Jurgen sounded puzzled.

"Is that a bad thing?" Clive could see the worn track and that they definitely weren't on it.

Jurgen made a sound that was neither yes or no.

"What's her name?"

"Linda with Thor," as if it was a single name.

Clive couldn't stop the laugh. "*That* scruffy little mutt is named Thor?"

Jurgen's grin would look appropriately nasty to be carved into the flesh of a Halloween pumpkin.

The woman had transformed once she started the course. Pretty and intent had transformed to focused to the point of lethal. She moved with all the efficiency of a fine-honed knife blade. Maybe she was Thor and the dog was Linda.

Keep reading. Available at fine retailers everywhere.
Find it now!

ABOUT THE AUTHOR

M.L. Buchman started the first of, what is now over 50 novels and as many short stories, while flying from South Korea to ride his bicycle across the Australian Outback. Part of a solo around the world trip that ultimately launched his writing career.

All three of his military romantic suspense series—The Night Stalkers, Firehawks, and Delta Force—have had a title named "Top 10 Romance of the Year" by the American Library Association's *Booklist*. NPR and Barnes & Noble have named other titles "Top 5 Romance of the Year." In 2016 he was a finalist for Romance Writers of America prestigious RITA award. He also writes: contemporary romance, thrillers, and fantasy.

Past lives include: years as a project manager, rebuilding and single-handing a fifty-foot sailboat, both flying and jumping out of airplanes, and he has designed and built two houses. He is now making his living as a full-time writer on the Oregon Coast with his beloved wife and is constantly amazed at what you can do with a degree in Geophysics. You may keep up with his writing and receive a free starter e-library by subscribing to his newsletter at: www.mlbuchman.com

Join the conversation:

www.mlbuchman.com

Other works by M. L. Buchman:

SIGN UP FOR M. L. BUCHMAN'S NEWSLETTER TODAY

and receive:
Release News
Free Short Stories
a Free Book

Get your free book today. Do it now.
free-book.mlbuchman.com

CPSIA information can be obtained
at www.ICGtesting.com
Printed in the USA
FSHW04n1951280318
46309FS